PAL JOEY

The Novel and
The Libretto and Lyrics

PAL JOEY

The Novel by
John O'Hara

AND THE LIBRETTO AND LYRICS

Libretto by John O'Hara
Lyrics by Lorenz Hart
Music by Richard Rodgers

VINTAGE BOOKS
A DIVISION OF RANDOM HOUSE
NEW YORK

Library of Congress Cataloging in Publication Data
O'Hara, John, 1905-1970.
Pal Joey.
"The novel by John O'Hara and the libretto and lyrics,
libretto by John O'Hara, lyrics by Lorenz Hart,
music by Richard Rodgers."
Reprint. Originally published: New York:
Popular Library, 1976.
I. Hart, Lorenz, 1895-1943.
II. Rodgers, Richard, 1902-   . Pal Joey. Libretto. 1983.
III. Title.
PS3529.H29P34 1983   813'.52   82-40417
ISBN 0-394-71188-2

The Novel

PAL JOEY

Pal Joey

DEAR PAL TED:

Well at last I am getting around to knocking off a line or two to let you know how much I apprisiate it you sending me that wire on opening nite. Dont think because I didnt answer before I didnt apprisiate it because that is far from the case. But I guess you know that because if you knew when I was opening you surely must be aware how busy Ive been ever since opening nite. I figure you read in *Variety* what date I was opening in which case I figure you have seen the write ups since then telling how busy Ive been and believe me its no exagerton.

Well maybe it seems a long time since opening nite and in a way it does to me too. It will only be five weeks this coming Friday but it seems longer considering all that has happened to your old pal Joey. Its hard to believe that under two months ago Joey was strictly from hunger as they say but I was. The last time I saw you (August) remember the panic was on. I figured things would begin to break a little better around August but no. A couple spots where I figured I would fit in didnt open at all on acct of bankroll trouble and that was why I left town and came out this way. I figured you live in a small town in Michigan and you can stay away from the hot

spots because there arent any and that way you save
money. I was correct but I sure didnt figure the panic
would stay on as long as it did. I finely sold the jalloppy
and hocked my diamond ring the minute I heard
there would be a chance down this way. I never was
in Ohio before but maybe I will never be any place
else. At least I like it enough to remain here the remainder
of my life but of course if NBC is listening
in Im only kidding.

Well I heard about this spot through a little mouse
I got to know up in Michigan. She told me about this
spot as it is her home town altho spending her vacation
every year in Michigan. I was to a party one nite
(private) and they finely got me to sing a few numbers
for them and the mouse couldn't take her eyes
off me. She sat over in one corner of the room not
paying any attention to the dope she was with until
finely it got so even he noticed it and began making
cracks but loud. I burned but went on singing and
playing but he got too loud and I had to stop in the
middle of a number and I said right at him if he
didnt like it why didnt he try himself. Perhaps he
could do better. The others at the party got sore at
him and told him to pipe down but that only made
him madder and the others told me to go ahead and
not pay any attention to him. So I did. Then when I
got finished with a few more numbers I looked
around and the heel wasnt there but the mouse was.
She didnt give me a hand but I could tell she was
more impressed than some that were beating their
paws off. So I went over to her and told her I was
sorry if it embarrassed her me calling attenton to her
dope boyfriend but she said he wasnt a boyfriend. I
said well I figured that. I said she looked as if she
could do better than him and she said "you for in-

stance" and I said well yes. We laughed and got along
fine and I took her home. She was staying with her
grandmother and grandfather, two respectible old
married people that lived there all their life. They
were too damn respectible for me. They watched
her like a hawk and one oclock was the latest she
could be out. That to me is the dumbest way to treat
that kind of a mouse. If its going to happen it can
happen before nine oclock and if it isnt going to happen it isnt going to no matter if you stay out till nine
oclock the next morning. But whats the use of being
old if you cant be dumb? So anyway Nan told me
about this spot down here and knew the asst mgr of
the hotel where the spot is and she said she would
give me a send in and if I didnt hold them up for too
much of the ready she was sure I could get the job. I
sing and play every afternoon in the cocktail bar and
at night I relieve the band in the ballroom. Anyway
I figured I would have to freshen up the old wardrobe
so I had to get rid of the jalloppy and hock my diamond ring. I made the trip to Ohio with Nan in her
own jalloppy which isn't exactly a jalloppy I might
add. Its a 37 Plymouth conv coop. It took us three
days to go from Mich. to Ohio but Ill thank you not
to ask any questions about my private life.

This asst mgr auditioned me when we finely arrived and I knew right away I was in because he
asked me for a couple of old numbers like Everybody
Step and Swanee and a Jerry Kern medley and he
was a Carmichael fan. Everything he asked me for I
gave him and of course I put up a nice appearance
being sunburned and a white coat from the proseeds
of selling the jalloppy and hocking the ring. I re-
hearsed with the band altho Collins the leader hates

my guts and finely I talked this asst mgr into letting me do a single irregardless of the band and he did.

Well you might say I ran the opening nite. I m.c'd and they had a couple of kids from a local dancing school doing tap, one of them not bad altho no serious competition for Ginger Rogers. They were only on for the first week. They also had another mouse who was with the band, living with the drummer. She tried to be like Maxine. Well she wasnt even colored, thats how much like Maxine she was. The local 400 turned out for the opening nite and inside a week I was besieged with offers to entertain at private parties which I do nearly every Sunday as the bar and ballroom are not open Sunday or at least I do not work. In additon to the job at the hotel and the private parties you probably have read about the radio job. I went on sustaining the first week and by the end of the second week I got myself a nice little commercial. I am on just before the local staton hooks up with NBC Blue Network five nites a week but I dont think you can catch me in New York. Not yet! My sponsor is the Acme Credit Jewellery Compay but I only have eight more weeks to go with them then I am free to negosiate with a better sponsor. Still Im not complaining. Your old pal Joey is doing all right for himself. I get a due bill at the hotel and what they pay me in additon aint hay. I also have the radio spot and the private parties. I went for a second hand Lasalle coop and I am thinking of joining the country club. I go there all the time with some of the local 400 so I figure I might as well join but will wait till I make sure I am going to stay here. I get my picture in the paper and write ups so much that I dont even bother to put them in my scrap book any more. The crowd at the club are always ribbing me about it and accuse

me of having the reporters on my payroll but I just
tell them no, not the reporters, the editors. I am a
little sore at one of the papers because the local Winchell links my name constantly with the name of a
very sweet kid that I go to the club and play golf
with. Not that it isnt true. We see each other all the
time and she comes to the hotel practically every
nite with a party and when Im through for the nite we
usely take a ride out to a late spot out in the country.
Her father is the president of the second largest bank.
It is the oldest. The biggest bank was formally two
banks but they merged. Her name is Jean Spencer
and a sweeter kid never lived. I really go for her.
But this local Winchell took a personal dislike to me
and made a couple cracks about us. One was "That
personality boy at a downtown hotel has aired the
femme that got him the job and is now trying to
move into society." Me trying to move in to society!
Society moved in on me is more like it. Jean was
burned because she was afraid her father might see
the item and when I meet her father I dont want him
to have the wrong impression. I think the colyumist
got the item from my ex-friend Nan. I didnt see much
of her when I was rehearsing and the afternoon of
opening nite she called up and said she wanted to
come but what the hell could I do? Ask for a big table
when they were getting $5 a head cover charge? I
was glad enough to get the job without asking too
many favors. Then a week or so later she called up
and asked me could I let her have $50. I asked her
what for and she hung up. Well if she didnt even
want to do me the curtesy to tell me what for I
wasnt going to follow her around begging her to take
it. But I gave it a few days thought and decided to
let her have it but when I phoned her they said she

quit her job and left town. I understand from Schall the asst mgr that she sold her Plymouth and went to N.Y. Her name is Nan Hennessey so if you run into her anywhere youll know her. She could be worse, that is worse on the eye, a little dumb tho.

Well pally, they will be billing me for stealing all their writing paper if I dont quit this. Just to show you I dont forget I inclose $30. Ill let you have the rest as soon as possible. Any time I can help you out the same way just let me know and you can count on me. I guess you kissed that fifty goodbye but that isnt the way I do things. But I guess you know that, hey pal?

All the best from
PAL JOEY

Ex-Pal

DEAR FRIEND TED:

That is if I can call you friend after the last two weeks for it is a hard thing to do considering. I do not know if you realize what has happen to me oweing to your lack of consideraton. Maybe it is not lack of consideraton. Maybe it is on purpose. Well if it is on purpose all I have to say is maybe you are the one that will be the loser and not me as I was going to do certan things for you but now it does not look like I will be able to do them.

Let us rehearse the whole thing briefley. I wrote to you on the 26 or 7 of last month telling you how I was getting along and inclosing $30 and telling you all the news out here about me getting this radio job and singing in the hotel. Also telling you I was going around with a girl in the local 400 who had a father a banker et cetra. Then I also made the unfortunate error of telling you to look up a certan mouse if you happen to come across her. Which you did and mentoned my name. Well theres the rub. Oweing to your lack of consideraton (mentoning my name) there is hell to pay and I will tell you why. Maybe you know why. Maybe you knew damn well what you were doing and maybe not but anyhow I will tell you just in case.

The way I get it you meet this mouse and right off you shoot off your face about I wrote you and told you to look her up and she gets the wrong impression because as I understand it she thinks you think all you have to do is menton my name and you are in. Then she gets sore as hell and decides to get even with me. Well here I am 1000 miles from N. Y. and doing OK with my radio job and singing at the hotel and with this kid that has a father a banker and out of the blue everything goes haywire. You knew damn well the mouse I told you about was from this town because I remember distintly telling you all about her in my letter of the 26 or 7. I remember distintly telling you she was no tramp and you only drew your own conclusons and not from anything I told you. So here I am doing OK with a car and two good jobs and this society kid going for me and what happens. This is what happens. I do not know what because it is too earley to say.

First of all the asst mgr of the hotel where I am singing he comes to me and says "Joey I just rec'd informaton that is not doing you any good around this town and I want you to level with me and tell me if it is true." What? I said. What informaton? "Well I do not exactly know how to put it man to man. We are both men of the world but this is what I have reference to, meaning that a certain mouse from this town had to leave town on acc't of you and is now in N.Y. and instead of helping her you are writing letters to pals in N. Y. and shooting off your face about what a don Juan you are. That dont do you any good personally and I will state frankly that while we are highly pleased with your singing and drawing power as a personality here at the hotel however we have to look at it from all the angels and once it gets around that you are the kind of chap that writes letters to his pals in N. Y. mentoning his fatal attracton to the ladies why some nite some guy is just going to get his load on and you are singing and a guy will walk up and take a poke at you while you are singing. Think it over" he said. Well this asst mgr is a pal of mine and I have the deepest respect for him and I went on & did a couple numbers and after I went to him and got him to tell me all about it. In detail.

So you call yourself a pal. Well that mouse I told you to look up knew this asst mgr in fact I think I told you she introduce me to him. I can see it all clearly. You met her and moved in and then you told her I told you all about her and the little trip we took on the way down from Michigan. As if that wasnt enough the next thing you do you have to destroy the only fine decent thing that has happen to me since coming to this jerk town, namely Jean. Jean is the girl that has a father a banker and it was only a queston of time before I was to meet the family and from there it was only a queston of time before things came to the definitely serious stage, but boy you certanly louse that up. I was to accompany Jean to a private party last Tues. nite and she would pick me up at the hotel after I did a couple numbers and go to this party. Usully when she picks me up she is with another couple but last Tues. when the doorman sent in word she was there she was alone in her Packard conv coop. I thought nothing of it till I noticed she was not driving in the direcpton of this private party and also not opening her trap but just driving and I called her attenton to the fact. "No. We are not going to Dwight and Connie Reynolds party this evening" she said. I thought maybe it was called off and said so but she said no it was not called off but she wanted to

talk with me. Then out it came. Thanks to you she
gets this annonamous letter from that mouse I told
you about saying to look out for me that I was a guy
that would move in on her and then shoot off my face
about it all over. I ask her if I could see the letter and
she said she tore it up and I said did she look at the
postmark. "Was it postmark N. Y.?" I said. She said
no, here, but of course that mouse would send it to
some girl friend here and get it postmark here. Well
Jean & I had quite a scene much as I dislike scenes
and no am't of persuason on my part would convince
her it was the work of a lousy bitch that all she was
was jealous. "To think that I was on the vurge of in-
viting you to Sunday dinner next Sunday she said.
That shows how things stood between she & I, but so
that is all loused up too.

Well I was frantic. I had come to care deeply for
Jean. She lives in a very different world than you and
I. Her father is this banker and very conservative and
not use to having his daughter going around with
chaps that sing in a hotel even if it is one of the prin-
ciple hotels in the mid west. I go out with all the best
people here the 400 but not the older crowd & just on
the vurge of going to Jeans house for Sunday dinner
she gets this annonamous letter sticking the shiv in
my back. Thanks to you. Well I thought for a minute
maybe the mouse came home & sent the letter herself and I gave her a buzz Wed. afternoon and a
dame's voice answered and when she said who was it
I told her and it turned out to be the sister of the one
that is causeing all the trouble. When I told her who
I was she called me everything she could think of till
I thought if anybody was listening in they would
think they were overhearing some bag and that she
probably is because you got to be a bag to know

some of the things she called me. She also made
threats and said one of these nites she was coming
down to the hotel when I was doing a number and
would personally spit in my eye and knock me the
hell off the stand. Then I told her what I thought of
her *and* her sister and if she ever showed her face
around the hotel I would knock her teeth down her
throat. Woman or no woman. I shut her up the bitch.
I said she and her fine feathered sister. Well I said if
she wanted to know anything about her sister ask
anybody that was in Michigan last summer and she
would find out what I meant. So if you see the mouse
again you can tell her. I dont give a damn if I lose my
job here at the hotel or the radio spot. I dont have to
take that stuff from any mouse or her sister. As for
you my ex-pal you know what you can do and also
you can sing for the $20 I owe you. I am making a
little trip to N.Y. in the near future and we will have
a little talk and you can explain your positon, altho
the way I feel now if I saw you now your positon
would be horizontle. I might as well tell you I am going to the gym 3 or 4 times a week and not that I
need it because I always could slap you around
when ever I wanted to.

You know what you can do.

YOUR EX-PAL JOEY

How I Am Now in Chi

PAL TED:

Well, pally, I have come to the concluson that old pals are best and never put too much faith in new acquaintances or you will end up two away from the 9 ball. When I tell you that you are getting it straight from head-quarters, because I know. I have been thinking it over and the true test of friendship is if you can weather such things as for instance you and I, meaning like differences of opinon over a mouse or the dough department and things on that order. You and I certanly have had our differences of opinon over the above yet here I am when I think it over and give the matter mature consideraton I think of you as a friend and I always hope you will consider me a friend if you have the ill fortune of ever getting in a spot in which I found myself recently. Then you can count on me altho' hoping the occason does not arise. (God forbid.)

Well I recall telling you about a little mouse one of the local 400 that her father was president of the bank (largest in town). This mouse Jean by name use to come every night to the hotel to hear me sing and it got so it was embarrasing owing to the fact that those lugs in the band would begin to kid me about it. They would say that mouse has got it for Joey but bad. She would come there and sit and just look at me and when she would get up to dance and I would sing she would just stand there in front of me with her escort and it became so that it was obvious and altho' I pride myself on being equal to such situatons (having had the experience before) it use to disconcert me more than I can say. However she arranged an introducton and I use to take her out especially when I was singing at private parties of the local 400. In a short time she use to stop for me at the hotel damn near every evening and I came to care for her as she was different than the usual ones that make a fool of themselves over a singer or entertainer. We were reaching the stage where it was you might say only a queston of time before Joey and Jean would veil up and perhaps I would consider giving up this life. Not that I ever intended doing that but she use to discuss it with me. She often use to ask me if I thought my life interesting and was it fun and how did I happen to get in it and of course that was her subtle way of getting me to consider probably going into the banking game with her father after we got married.

Well of course she was nineteen years old and one for the book as far as looks, figure, personality is concerned and also had plenty of scratch, being the bank presidents daughter. I went to work and bought a couple new arrangements in fact she gave me one for Xmas last Xmas. I happen to say one night I needed a couple new arrangements and she asked me how much they were and I told her my guy charged $50. She also gave me a set of studs and cuff links to wear with my tails that must have set her back the price of four arrangements. It was her favorite song at the time, the arrangement she gave me. It was You go to my Head. I had an old arrange-

ment of it from last summer but never had any call
for it but she use to like it before she met me and so I
got out the old arrangement and of course did not
spoil it for her by saying it was one I had last summer
and never had any call for. However I used the 50 to
give her a Xmas present, a sport watch.

Then around the end of January they were having
this ball in honor of the President (Roosevelt) to get
up a fund that they would give for this infantile pa-
ralasys. Very white of them as they sit around all year
and say what a heel he is and on his birthday they
give him this ball and it is a club called the Junior
League that she belonged to had charge of getting
the talent and all that like publicity etc. So of course
I gladly donated my services as I was going anyway
having planned to escort Jean to the ball. The ball
was in the ballroom of the hotel but I was going to
escort her from her house. Then at the very last minute I said to her what should we do that evening until
it was time to go to the ball (11.30 or 12) and she
said she was going to a dinner party at these friends
of hers named Fenton. I said it was a fine time to tell
me that and said I consider it a fine thing to go to the
Fenton's for dinner knowing that they were one of the
few that took a snobbish attitude in connecton
with me. I told her she could take it or leave it and if
she went to their house for dinner she could count me
out on the subject of escorting her to the ball. I was
plenty burned and she said she never understood I
was taking her anyway and of course she was right.
I took it for granted and didnt bother to ask her until
the last minute and then I said well I will just stop
for you at the Fenton's about 11.30 and that will save
you the trouble of coming to the ball alone or with
another couple. Imagine my surprise to learn that she

already had an escort, Jerry Towle a young dope that does nothing but fly his own plane and scaring farmer's horses and always in some kind of jam with the law but his old man has plenty of scratch and gets him out of it. I said you go with Towle and let him take you every other place from now on and I said dont bother to come to the hotel any more but stay away and our date for the next night was off.

Well we had a quarrel about that and it ended up I didn't go to the Fenton's and when I was singing that night at the ball she made Towle dance her up and request Go to my Head but I said very politely I only had the newer numbers and did not sing Go to my Head this year. Did she burn? I didnt even dance with her and I only sat with the boys in the band all night and then went up to my room after I did my numbers and called up some hustler and took her to a hamburger joint where the 400 go every night after dances and hoped Jean and Towle would come in but they never did so I gave the hustler 5 bucks for her time and sent her home in a taxi.

Well the next night I am singing and in she comes but I never give her a tumble but she gets her load on I notice and about one a.m. a note comes over by waiter and she wants me to meet her but she is with this party and I am burned so I dont answer the note. I just tell the waiter no reply and when I finish my last number I screw and go around the corner to have a cup of coffee and there she is, followed me. I do not want to make a scene then and there and she has her load on and will not go back and rejoin her party so I send around and get my car out of the garage hoping to take her for a ride and sober her up but oh no. Instead we go for a ride and altho' it was freezing and we did not have a coat either of us we are out for about an hour and always fighting and it began to get late and I knew the grill at the hotel would be putting the chairs up on the tables so I ignored her and turned around and went back. No sign of her party. They have gone. That means I have to take her home and she lives out in the suburbs and by the time we get there somebody has called her up to see if she got home and woke up the old man and he is waiting for her in a dressing gown. She is still plastered the little lush and her old man asks what the meaning of this is and who am I and bringing his daughter home in this conditon. Then I tell him who I am and he says Oh, he has heard about me and has always wanted to meet me and without any warning brings one up from the floor and I stop it with my chin, as dirty a punch as I ever saw. I got up but had the presence of mind so that I did not let him have one but said I dont want any part of his daughter, the lush. Keep her home or he would be a grandfather one of these days without a son in law. I think he would have got a gun but I was out of there before he had the chance.

Well the next a.m. about 10 the phone rings and it is the manager, my boss. He wants me down in his office so I go and he hears all about it only an exageraton of what really happened. To make a long story short I am out. I say what about my contract and he says read your contract and then I remember he had the right to fire me if I get out of line and he gives me the rest of the week (pay) and an extra week and says he advised me to lam out of there as I insulted the most powerful man in the whole town as I will soon find out. I find out alright. I call up this ad agency that pays me for singing on the local radio staton where my sponsor is this credit jewelry company. They

were just about to call me. I am out. The mouse's old
man only owns the God damn staton. I go to a law-
yer but he wont take my case as he says I havent any
case. Even if I had he would think twice about buck-
ing this mouse's old man. So there I am holding an
empty bag with my wardrobe and a car only about
half paid for and all told about a little over 300 in my
kick. So I go back to the hotel and start in packing
(about 5 in the afternoon this is) and a messenger
comes and brings me a note from Jean. She is sorry
about it and did not want to cause me all this trouble
and would do anything to make or mend. Her old
man had her at the doctor's or she would have got in
touch with me sooner and will I call her at this number, a girl friend of hers. They are going to take her
to some place in N. Carolina the next day and she
has to see me. I do not have to worry as the dr. says
she is okay, but she would not be able to stand it going like this with me feeling this way all over a little
thing like a misunderstanding over the Fenton's
dinner and she heard her old man threaten to get me
bounced out of town etc and she is desperate because
she loves me. Well I thought it over and what a fine
chance I had to show her old man who was the most
powerful man in town as far as his own family are
concerned. All I had to do was pick up Jean and drive
over the state line and inside of two hours he would
have a son in law alright. I am sitting there debating
within myself as to whether I will call her or not and
the door opens. "You know me," he says. Towle. "I
see you are packing. Good. There is a 9 oclock for
Chicago and an 8.30 for N. Y. and I would suggest
the 8.30 but I leave the choice entirely up to you,"
he says. "I think I will sit around and take you to the
train." I ignore him but go on packing and when I

finish up I send down and have room service bring
me up a steak sandwich with French fries, a cup of
coffee and a piece of pie and I eat it there with him
sitting there. I had to pay cash for it as room service
will not let me sign. Then I lit a butt and smoke it
calmly and then I phone the railroad and order a
lower on the 9 oclock for Chi. I can see he is burned
but that is what I intend. Then the phone rings and
he answers it and says he is not here but has just left
and then he says "Dont be a damn fool Jean this is
Jerry and yes he is here but you are not going to see
him if I can help it and you may not speak to him as
I am acting on your fathers orders." Then he hangs
up. He is a big lug. Over 200.

Well I phone the garage and tell them to put my
car into dead storage and take out the battry and then
it is time to go to the train and he goes with me.
When we get there I tell him he can have the pleasure of paying the taxi and he says it is a pleasure
alright and I said I thought it would be and also a pleasure for me. When I go to get my ticket he even pays
for the ticket, tips the porter, etc. I did not lose my
sense of humor. I said "By the way I have nothing to
read on the train" and he buys me papers and maga-
zines. I see the humor in it and I also say I always
have chewing-gum on trains so he buys me some gum.
But he does not see the humor for when the train is
ready to pull out I reach out my hand and say it was
a pleasure to have him come down and see me off,
him of all people and just then he hauls off and slaps
my hand, burned like I never saw anybody burned.

Well the train pulled out and that is the story of
how I am now in Chi. I am singing for coffee & cakes
at a crib on Cottage Grove Ave. here. It isnt much of
a spot but they say it is lucky as four or five singers

and musicians who worked here went from here to big things and I am hoping. Well give my best to Artie and Fred and Chink and Mort. Tell Mort congratulations as I hear he is starting up a new band and I would be willing to work for scale. Tell Fred when he comes out to look me up as I plug his last two numbers every nite. Well Ted all the best and I don't have to say I think your solo in Jeepers Creepers is as good as Vanuti. I am glad a pal is having such good luck and I mean that sincerely as ever. Will write soon again.

PAL JOEY

Bow Wow

DEAR FRIEND TED:

Well pal I had to sit down the minute I came home just returning from a furniture store around the corner from where I am living. Having just heard what you did to Hong Kong Blues. Well if I was ever proud of a friend I am proud of you alright. To say it is a wonderful recording is to say the least. I happen to drop in at this store as I do every week to hear the new recordings. You know me, Ted. Strictly larceny when it comes to listening to those arrangements but I cant afford to buy any new arrangements of my own right now so I have to get them from recordings and take the best of this one and that one. The joint where I am singing and m. c-ing in is satisfied with my work and it keeps me in coffee & cakes but not much more. As a pal of mine said the other night Chicago is alright if you like Chicago altho I would rather be back in N. Y. or even go to Frisco for the other Fair. I have had one or two propositons in regards to Frisco but nothing attractive. That is to make it worth while going all the way out there and then maybe getting stuck where I dont know anybody. I dont know what to do so for the moment am sticking here getting my coffee & cakes and building up a local following. They have a place out on the North side that has made me

one or two offers but I will stay down in this territory
until I get a propositon from some place in the Loop
dist. I figure I ought to go good in a place like the
Chez Paris, tops here, or maybe one of the hotels.
Downey always goes good here altho his stuff is of
course different than mine. Well enough of my prob-
lems. I only wanted to conveigh my congratulatons
on the new recordings and for a young band. Who
have you got on the guitar? If I didn't know Mc-
Donough was dead I would say it was him. I also
thought I recognized Fud but I guess he is still with
Tommy so guess I am an error.

Well I guess you wonder what I do with my spare
moments out in this bailwick. Write letters is one
thing. Just think a year ago you were the one crying
the blues and less than a year ago I was doing alright
with the Packard etc. And now you are up there and
there will be no stopping you and believe me you
have the ardent wishes of success from all your pals.
I am getting by in this crib in Chi. but guess I have
learned my lesson and am a changed man. All because of a dog.

Well this is the first time I wrote since I bo't Skippy
the name of my dog and it is wonderful what they can
do. They give you the courge to continue when things
look bad. I use to hear Al White on the subject of
man's best friend the dog and use to laugh myself
sick when White would rib the love and affecton of a
man and a dog but he is wrong. There is something
to it. It worked in my case as when I came out here
I didnt have any job and took the first thing that came
along and took the attitude that the world was a
pretty sorry place to live in and it effected my work.
I would get up to do a number and I took the attitude
that I hated all the people there and I guess it showed

because Lang (no relaton to Eddie) the owner of this spot gave me a call. He said get more of a pleasing personality in it or pack. It put the fear of God in me as I wasnt there long enough to build up a following and had not stashed any dough away. Also no prospects or propositons from other spots and of course this joint dont spend any dough advertising and the press agent gets no pay but only a certan am't of drinks on the cuff so you can imagine how hard he works. So I gave the matter my mature consideraton and then that week I was out getting my breakfast around 4 one afternoon and right near where I eat is this pet & dog shop. I never had any interest in dogs and never considered owning one and thought they were a nusaince especially in towns. But I saw this mouse standing there bent over and talking to one of the dogs in the window of the shop. She was about twenty and I didn't care if she had a face out of the Zoo but spring was in the air and this mouse had a shape that you dont see only on the second Tuesday of every week and when you do see a shape like that you have to do something about it. So I stopped and feined an interest in the dog kingdom and cased the mouse and got a look at her kisser. Well it fitted in with the rest of the body. Not pretty but cute. She had personality in her face I could see that. She didn't see me because she was so crazy about this one dog that had his nose up against the window and she was talking to it before she noticed me and then got sort of embarassed when she saw me. But by that time I was looking at the dog and smiling at him and leaned over and started talking and the first name I could think of came to my head and I said hello Skippy boy. And the mouse looked at me and said is that his name, Skippy? I said I didnt know I only pre-

tend it was. I said I pass by here every day and got
to love him so much that I had to give him a name
like the name of an airdale dog I used to have when
I was a kid. Oh so I love dogs, she wanted to know
and I said yes. Then she said why didnt I buy this
puppy and I said for the same reason why I didnt buy
a Dusenburg, money. Well the effect it had on her
was wonderful. I could see tears in her eyes and she
said it was a shame that anybody that love dogs
so much had to be deprived of them because of the
finances where so many people that didnt really love
them had them and didnt treat them properly. Yes,
I said, that is true. I said I was saving up so I could
buy Skippy and there was a sign in the window that
said $30. That part was the truth, that is, I didnt have
any $30 to buy any dogs with. I began telling her
about Skippy the airdale that I didnt have when I
was a kid and pretty soon got to believing it myself,
all about how my heart was broken when poor little
Skippy was crushed beneath the wheels of a 10 ton
truck. I said my family were well to do people in
those days and wished to buy me another dog but I
said to them no dog would take the place of Skippy
and never would until one day I happen to be going
by this shop and my eye caught this little puppy's
and something about him reminded me of Skippy
and she said yes, he was a little like an airdale. Well
I didnt know a airdale from a hole in the ground and
didnt know what the hell this mut was in the window
and so I said it wasnt the breed, I said, it was just
something in this puppy's expresson that reminded
me of my old Skippy. She was touched. She said she
never would of taken me for somebody that loved
dogs so much and I said you dont know much about
dogs then, Miss. I said dogs have strange tastes in

people and only a dog knows who he likes. By this
time Skippy was laying down and I said he is tired
and I said I had to go and get my breakfast. I said this
is the only time of the day that I can see Skippy as
they take them out of the window soon. Just a guess
but I didnt seem to remember seeing the dogs in the
window late in the afternoon and the mouse said
"Did I hear correctly when you said you were going
to have breakfast?" And I said yes, I am one of
those unusual people that their days are upside down.
I said you are probably the kind that would be having
tea now but I am having breakfast. That made her
laugh and so I took advantage of that and said why
not have tea with me if she didnt mind sitting at a
counter for it? As I said before I had cased this mouse
and she was pretty but I knew she was no society
debutante. Probably a stenog out of work but very
cute. So she said she often ate at counters and went
with me. I was right and she was a stenog looking for
work. She went with me to this one-arm where I eat
and she had a tomato on rye and a coffee and I had
eggs and coffee and we started talking and it turned
out she was from some little town in Illinois, not
Peoria but some place like it. Her name was Betty
Hardiman and lived with her married sister and her
husband and only came to Chi a month before. I
told her my people lost all their money in the crash
and I had to leave Princeton college and go to work
but the only work I was suited for was singing with a
band or in a night club and then she said she recognized my name from passing the club on her way to
the L. She said she thought people that worked in
clubs got plenty of money and I said it depends on
what club and then when it came time to pay the
check she said she would pay her own and insisted

and said let me consider that her contributon to buying Skippy.

Well I said I hoped she would come around to the
club some time with her boy friend and I would sing
any number she would request and she said her
boy friend didnt live in Chi but went to college at the
Illinois U. at Champaign. I said well she should come
some time with her sister and her husband and Betty
said her bro. in-law never went to night clubs and I
said I guess it was pretty dreary for a young girl living like that and she said it was becoming that way
altho it was better than home. She said she loved
Chi, just going around the Loop and watching the
people's faces on the L trains. but would like to see
some more of the fun but her boy friend was working
his way thru the Illinois U. and didnt get to Chi only
two or three times a year. Well I said this is very
pleasant but I had to go and rehearse a couple numbers at the club and got her phone number and said
I would like to take her out some night if I got a night
off and she said she tho't it would be alright.

Well I saw her a couple times but only in the day
time. We use to meet at the dog shop. We would
go to the one-arm and then I would have to leave her
but one afternoon she borrowed her bro. in-law's car
and drove out to the country and I gave her a little
going over but not too much as I could tell the time
was not ripe. I was even surprised I could neck her
at all on acc't of this boy friend at the Illinois U. but
I guess it was the first time a pass was made at her
since the last time she saw the college boy and I guess
she needed a little work-out. Well that night I hit a
crap game for about eighty clams and two days later
I met Betty and told her and she said now I could

buy Skippy and I said no, unfortunately the flea-bag where I was living did not permit dogs. I said that was just my luck. Then I said I have an idea. I said how about if I buy him for her and she could keep him on conditon that she would let me see him and she said she would love to but would have to ask her sister as they only had an apartment. I met the sister by that time and I knew she went for me but had not met the bro. in-law. She asked the sister but the sister said no, Betty couldn't have a dog in the ap't because it was too small, much as she would love to have a dog. So then I went to my landlady and asked her if I could have a dog and she said sure so then I went to Betty and told her I had a deal with my landlady that if I paid more rent I could keep the dog so Betty was overjoyed and I bo't Skippy. The landlady has a kid about ten or eleven and he takes care of Skippy for me. Takes him for his walks and washes him and the landlady thinks I am a fine young fellow but why shouldnt she when her kid has the use of a $30 dog for nothing. I often have fun with the mut too and pat him and I often think if it wasn't for Skippy I never would of met Betty. Her sister and bro. in-law are going away the week-end after next and we will have the ap't all to ourselves. It's about time but I had to be patient as she said she wanted to be sure first, but a man with such a love and affecton for dogs was a man you could trust. Well, pal, all the best and keep your eyes open for any spots you hear for me. I would rather be around N.Y. this summer as it gets hot as hell out here in summer but if you hear anything like a good spot with a band touring or some summer hotel in Mass. or Maine dont forget your pal. I have no contract here as they never heard of a contract at a crib like this so can leave at a moment's notice. Of course it will be worth sticking around a month or so if you get what I mean. Bow wow.

PAL JOEY

Avast and Belay

FRIEND TED:

Well, chum, still in Chi, doing alright and have my notices to prove it like one critic that I hardly know at all that works on a throwaway that they distribute at hotels etc. but is far the best writer on the nite life and he goes on to say I am the smoothest and most urbane singer of sophisticated melodies this town has seen in many a moon, and it was not a case of me taking an ad to get the write-up as the 1st I knew of it was when somebody showed it to me. "What is he your cousin?" said one of the lightweights in the band as he ignore the band and just gave them a menton in passing and devoted all his write-up to me. I only menton this now because I have in mind an idea that I want to discuss with you in this letter.

Well, chum, this is the idea I have been taking under consideraton and the pro's & con's ever since around the beginning of Sept. but more so lately owing to a conversaton I had with another chap recently. You would not know the name if I told you but his name is Charley Goas. Charley is a man around 40 odd yrs of age and a mind like a steel trap and knows all the angles. He is still alive today but use to be a big accountaint for Capone or one of the big mobs out

here like Capone or perhaps it was Bugs Moran or
Deeny O'bannon or Collosimo. I never asked him
that as he was not a mob guy himself but just did their
accountaincy for them and I would not know that
only I happen to ask somebody what he did and they
told me. I think he owns a piece of the room where
I sing in now but I am not suppose to know that and
do not pipe. Well he took a liking to me and drops
in every nite and we struck up an aquantainceship
and I guess he more or less considers me like a kid
bro. as he often gives me advice like on more than
1 occason he saw me looking at a mouse and when I
looked at him he smiled and without me saying anything he said to me, "That's for you, eh? O.K. sonny
boy if you want to end up on crutches." So that shows
how he took an interest in me and I apprisiate it and
therefore when he offered me some other advise I
also took it or am starting to take it by giving you this
idea I have in my mind.

This is the set-up. Charley was telling me one nite
how it looked like a sure thing there was going to be a
war. Next day, they declare war, and there was a ru-
mor around that the room would fold because business stank but I happen to know that Charley told the
backers they shouldnt be silly. They were ahead
enough so they could take a few bad nites and if
business didnt pick up why then fold but dont fold
until they saw if business was going to stay stinking
or perhaps get better. Charley was right. We kept
open and business is better than ever.

So all during this I got a chance to talk to Charley
about the war and he got to remenissing about in the
last war. I do not know for a fact if he was in the
army or navy as with Charley you leave Charley do
the talking and never ask questions. However he

asked me what my plans were and I said I did not give it much tho't as I did not think we would be in it and time enough when we got in. "Don't be silly," said Charley. "We will be in it before the horses stop running at Hialeah." This came as rather a surprise to me but before I had the opportunity to discuss it with him he said pick your spots now and do not be a sucker and get drafted. Then they can put you where they want to but if you pick yr. spot now you can stay in it and he said "Not this bunch of plumbers but do you have a contact with a guy with a good band" and I said "yes" and mentoned you as one of my eldest friends and he said he heard of you and said flattering things about you on the air and said he never met you but caught you & the band somewhere and got the impresson you have a wonderful personality and I agreed with him extremely. Well he said I was a fool if I did not make some kind of a propositon with you like get you to join the navy. Wait a minute now and read it all before you think I am going wacky. He said if a jig band by the name of Jim Europe (probably his professional name) during 1917 could be a big success in Paris why not a fellow like you, a name band known from coast to coast on the air and by records. He said there was this jig name Jim Europe had a band and they just about ran Paris in the war and after it until somebody took a shot at Mr. Europe and that ended him. All those Parisienns went for the band too which is a handy thing in a war. Acc. to Charley they even made this jig a lieutenant in the U.S.A. and he was a regular officer with a snappy uniform and white guys had to salute him owing to him being an officer. Well if they did that they ought to do it for you. He said take for instant Sousa, John Phillips Sousa and I remember

him, the march king. My old lady used to never tire
of Sousa on the phonograph until in desperaton I
broke the damn records and my old man belted me
for it as he also use to listen to them altho he did not
know a note of music but was a son of a bitch for
finding the nearest bar if you pardon the gag. Well
Sousa had this big corny band all brass and what did
they do but make him a kind of an admiral. Stars
& Stripes For-ever and Shine Little Glow-worm was
the kind of stuff he played so you can write your own
ticket with your repretory. He didnt play good but
played loud and so my 1st suggeston is get more brass
and gradually expand the size of the band and if I
were you I would give the boot to that rum-pot you
have now and get yourself a real press agent that
could get yr. picture in the Life magazine and maybe
it would be a good idea to get navy uniforms and
also get up a few routines like Waring use to have.
Drills, only learn to march instead of those routines
with cocktail shakers etc. that Waring use to have. All
this is my idea not Charley's as he only contributed
the original tho't and I put my brain to work on what
you could do if I called yr. attenton to it.

I am not trying to tell you how to run yr. band as
you do alright without me and once in a while when
I tho't to myself Ted ought to do this or that I re-
frained from telling you as it is your band not mine.
However this war stuff is an angle you may not of
thought of.

I am only scratching the surface with these sugges-
tons and have many more that are on the same order
but better and these randam notes now are just sug-
gestons or hints but ought to get yr. mind running in
that directon. We could do big things and at the same
time be patriotic doing it. As I understand it we

ought to figure on just the regular pay which is of course naturlly way below scale as when you are working for Uncle Sam he never heard of scale but would pay $30 a month to the ones with the rank of private and only cigarette money to a leader like yourself but of course I guess it would be understood with the army or navy that you could do jobs and records and of course a big patriotic band would get all the cream if you start soon enough. I have a slogan "put your band on the bandwagon" before the others get hep. I say we all the time because I take for granted you would get me a pardon out of this joint Chicago if you decide I have a good idea. If you wanted to put me on the pay-roll now I could give this joint notice just by saying why dont you guys go take a flying etc. and take a powder out of here that day and be in N.Y. the next. A wire will do the trick Ted boy. I will level with you. I get an honest yard here and was only saying that for laughs when I told you I got $150 the way we all exagerate in this business. You could go on working while I talk to the Army and Navy guys and whichever offers us the best proposition you can be sure I will take that one. Then when war is declared we are in uniform and ready to go that nite. Maybe by that time you would consider me such a good mgr. that you would have me for your peace-time mgr. even before we get in the war. I would find out in advance (from Charley) when we are getting in the war and would book you into some big Bway spot in time so that nite when war is declared we would be there in our uniforms. Think of the flash, as they use to say in vaudeville days. The 1st Swing Band in Uniform! It would be plastered all over the papers and with the right handling I see you shaking hands with the President at the White

House, him congratulating you for being the 1st band
in kahki, altho I hope the navy gives us the better
proposition as for a band the navy has better toggery.

Well think it over Ted because Charley says the
time is getting short. Charley says before the hay-
burners stop running at Hialeah. John Phillips Sousa
was an old man so they had to make him an admiral
but admiral sounds too old for you so if we decide the
navy offers us the better propositon you could be a
Commander. I could be a Leutenant Commander.
One thing I will add to the informaton above which
is this. I am only kidding about telling these Chicago
guys where to head in and this is why. It is because
Charley says during the last war they had anywhere
from 10 to 50,000 sailors in Chi. believe it or not.
They had a training camp here for sailors and that
was as close as they got to getting their head shot off.
If they got their head shot off it would be in a crap
game amongst themselves or in a riding academy on
the South Side. I am more in favor of the navy but
of course will take the better propositon. "So get the
band aboard the bandwagon" Ted and I am ready
the moment you give the downbeat. Charley said a
band like this no doubt would be booked for liberty
bond engagements when they start selling liberty
bonds to the people. I tho't of an angle there and
asked Charley "Suppose we are booked into a town to
sell these liberty bonds for the government do we
get our percent. of the gross" but Charley said not
with Mr. Whiskers at the gate, nobody cuts in on Mr.
Whiskers. But it just shows I was looking out for our
interest. Also Charley may be wrong. He can be. He
thinks his wife doesnt like me and boy he is so
wrong.

Well Commander, avast and belay and all that sort of thing.

Your pal

Joey

P.S.: I also want to warn you Vallee was in the navy in the last war and may have a good in there so we have to work fast so he wont crab our act.

Joey on Herta

DEAR PAL TED:

Well Pal I suppose you did not hear that yrs. truly the undersigned and to-wit has manage to build up a following so that they are borrowing the money wherewith to enlarge the joint and take care of the bigger and higher class clintele which followed on the heels of when I put over "Waiter with the Water"? But it is good news that you are banging them right over every where you go. I hear nothing but the best reports of you and the band and it is no secret that when you played the Palomar in Los Angeles, for a fairly recent band you broke the house record. Maybe you did not break the Goodman or Artie Shaw record but they made their record with an establish band and of course you went in there with scarcely if any radio build-up and still did terrific business. I am sure you glorify in your success and believe me when I say nothing could make me happier than you being right up there where you belong and am sure will not change in regard to your old pals. Might like to know later developments on how I am doing. Well here goes.

I told you the details and how I got creamed out of the hotel spot in Ohio & came here and made this connecton. For a while I was from hunger but suddenly clicked as it were over night. With me it was one of those things, just one of those crazy things. One nite singing a lung out for dopes that wouldn't know it if I was Toscanini, Al Rinker, or Brooks John or myself. All they cared about was if I sang Deep Purple 75 times a nite and they were satisfied. Female lushes that they would stand right under me while their escorts were giving them a little going over and I and the band were not suppose to see it. Oh no, just dumb, is what we were. I use to stand up there giving them Deep Purple and all the time the tho't kept cropping up in my mind "I only wish I had a water pistol, an old fashon water pistol such as we played with as a child and wouldn't I like to squirt you right in the eye with it Madam right in the mist of your memory Madam." But one nite I happen to get a small slice of Phil Harris broadcasting from Los Angeles and happen to tune in when he was polishing off Hold Tight. I said this can not be the guy that formerly I use to consider a road company Richman but it was. I knew there would be no trouble at all so I polished off his Hold Tight and practicly over nite I was the one man attracton of this joint. Then I caught Harris again one nite doing Fishes and from then on I and the joint were but set. The owner (only fronting for one of the many mobs they still got left here in Chi) gave me a quick hist in pay and began to talking contract but no said I. No contract now. Let's wait? (Meaning maybe some advertising agency might grab me off and did not want to be stuck with any contract.) So I let on like I was very happy at this joint & the only reason I was saying no contract was because I was coresponding with my agent in N. Y. and my hands were tied until hearing from him. That is a laugh, my agent. After they tied

a can to my tail in Ohio there wasnt an agent in the
U.S. that would give me a tumble. However that is
neither here nor there but is a sample. So they put
my name outside in lights and I was in but good.

Well I started out to tell you a little experience I
had which just goes to show you how the leaches
fasten upon a person practicly before they have time
to turn on the lights that spell out his name. This one
nite after I began clicking there was this large party
given by a bowling club consisting of people in the
neighborhood that belong to this neighborhood bowling club and met some nite every wk. in order to in-
dulge themselves in their silly pastime and this nite
was the nite when they had their annual get-together
for the purpose of the distributon of the awards &
prizes and of course they had about 40 or more there,
men & women. Well the press agent of this joint
said to me it would make a nice gesture if I would
make a few reference to this club when I introduced
my numbers and dedicate some numbers to them. He
kept talking about cagling. The only Cagle I ever
heard of was a football player that use to play for
West Point years ago but Cagling is also the name
for bowling so I made a few wise cracks about
Cagling that the p. a. gave me and I also put one of
my own in about Keg-lined beer cans altho why I
should give a plug to Bernie's ex-sponsor I do not
know only that it occured to me at the time. It went
over big and they liked me and soon were standing
around asking for request no's.

I happen to notice in the sea of faces this one kisser
that stood out in the crowd. About 21 and naturally
blonde hair and complected and most likely a Swede
I tho't. So then when they all insisted that I join
them I naturally obliged them and this mouse named

Herta Gersdorf was the one I gradually sat next to.
One word let to another and it turned out she would
like to be a singer and so to make a nice gesture to
the club and for good will etc. I said I have an an-
nouncement to make and Miss Herta Gersdorf will
sing. She pretend to be surprised but did not fool
me as I knew she was working on me to do that
very thing, so I brought her up to the mike and asked
her what she wanted to sing and what key but she did
not know what key, only the name of the song. Three
guesses. Day in Day Out. I encouraged her and got
her started and to my amazement she turned out to
have a voice not of course a trained voice and had no
experence in singing in public but I detected possibil-
ities in the voice and began to think to myself I had a
find. Well she got a big hand of course being a member of the cagle club and they did not detect the
rough edges and amateur touches or if they did they
forgave her owing to her youth and lack of experence
singing in public. So I helped her with an encore and
of course I made a lot of friends for the joint and also
increased my own following by the gesture. Well I
talked to her and inquired did she ever consider doing it professionally (singing I mean) and she said
she always use to dream of it but knew there was no
chance. So I said I would gladly help her and got
her phone no. and she said she would have to ask
her parents and the next day or 2 days later she called
me up and said they would like it if she could take
lessons from me but could not afford to pay anything and I said that would be o. k. So for a week I
went to her house every nite when she got home from
stenogging in the real estate office where she worked
and showed her a few things then after the 1st wk. I
brought her to the joint and late every afternoon I

would show her some mike technique and the differ-
ence between singing in front of a mike & without it.
She was a dumb little mouse but willing to learn. So
all the time I was thinking this was going to be my
favorite dish but at the time did not do anything
about it as I was being taken care of but too good by
a dame that had a little dress shop in the neighborhood. Anyway I never made a pitch with Herta. I
was afraid it would Herta. So what I did was find out
she was 21 and looked up an old agreement I had
with an agent the 1st time I ever had an agent and
copied it down and she signed it making me her agent
in case she clicked. Therefore I went to the "owner"
of the joint and said I had this mouse and told him
she was popular and had a voice which I was training and of course the 1st thing that heel did was he
said he wanted to warn me to watch my step and
dont get any bad reputaton in the neighborhood for
fooling around with the neighborhood kids or there
would be hell to pay and the patrons would stop
coming in imagine! I said to him he could let me
worry about my conduct, morals, etc and he said Oh
if there was any worrying to do I better do it which
sounded pretty sinistre but he was not throwing any
scare into me for I replied to him let us pass over
that phase of it and get down to business, did he or
did he not want this mouse she being under contract
to me in a strictly business legitamite deal and
showed him the contract. I said acting as artists representative for the girl I wanted $35 a wk. for her ser-
vices and we dickered until he came up to 25 and
then I said its a deal so I swung the job for her. It was
about time something like that happen to me after all
the hard luck I been having and also it was about
time Herta was getting around to paying something

on acc't as she never paid me a nickel for my instructon and lessons and rehearsals and my time, etc, and
her parents never offer to pay anything either so it
was a lucky thing for her I got her the job as it en-
abled her to pay me back $25 a wk. for the instructon
& time and lessons etc. and I was about to continue
giving her lessons while she worked. I shamed her
mother into getting up $30 for an evening dress. I
took one look at the dress they picked out for her and
said to them "May I inquire if you think Herta is singing for a choir?" I did not want to lose my temper
therefore the gag. The kid was built on the order of
Babs whatever her name was that worked with the
band when you use to play horn with Joe and here
they were trying to make her wear a dress for a con-
vent of sisters. So I entered into the situaton and informed them that I would take care of the clothes
dept. and out of my own pocket advanced her $9.50
so she could pour herself into a $39.50 no. that
showed everything but her scar where she had the
appendisetis if she ever had it (some spelling I admit). Also advanced her $5 to get her hair fixed up
and fingernails etc. Well I put her over but big and
she only fumbled one no. a little and I tho't at the
time after the 1st nite she was going to be grateful as
she seemed grateful at the time. I was of course going
on with the instructon etc. and let her have for nothing a couple arrangements I was thinking of polishing
off for myself. Also featured her in my own duets and
also gave her a swell break when I would introduce
her nos. I would introduce her as my protege Herta
(I dropped her last name but only used Herta like
Hildegard the singer that doesn't say her last name
either because it is some name from Milwaukee or
some place.) It went over. But little did I know.

Low and behold one nite before she went on she
said to me she had to be good that nite because her
boss & his wife would be there that nite. I said what
boss, forgetting. She meant the boss at the real estate
office where she stennoged. I forgot she was still
working there. So I gave her a big intro. and also
gave her 2 more nos to sing than usual so she could
impress her boss. Well I tho't no more of it till the
next nite she was there early & said she wanted to
talk to me and I said o.k. and what she wanted to
talk about was dough and I tho't being innocent I
tho't she wanted to pay me back the sums I advance to her but oh no. She said her boss asked her
how much she was getting and she told him our
arrangement about me coaching her etc. So the heel
went to the "owner" of the joint because he (Herta's
boss) handled the real estate deal on the property
and knew Lang, the "owner." He found out Lang
was giving me the 25 for Herta and so he wanted to
know why I didn't give her the 25 and put ideas in
her head that she should get the 25 less $2.50 for my
commission. $2.50!!! my commission for teaching her
everything she ever knew. Anyway I told her I said
I had a little matter of a contract and that stopped
her but the next nite who should come in but Martin the name of her boss and Lang was also there, just
before the joint opened for the nite. I do not wish to
bore you with the details but dont let anybody tell
you they got rid of the muscle boys in Chi. because
we argued pro & con and finally I got mad and
said I have a contract with Herta and Martin said
let me see it & I showed it to him and right before my
two eyes he slowly tore it up. He turn to Lang and
said "I guess everything is satisfactory now?" and
Lang laughed. I saw I was licked as those gorills do

not care anything about law and what was the use of me a stranger trying to do anything. Then I said "Mr. Martin just what is yr. angle?" Meaning what, he replied. I said "Oh nothing but I sure do admire yr. nerve." Oh my nerve is o. k. he said. I have nothing to fear from a punk crooner like you. I said with a smile "Go ahead and insult me as much as you care to, Mr. Martin, but I was not referring to that. All I was referring to was yr. nerve the way you bro't your wife here to hear the little girl friend the office wife sing." With that he burned and came at me but I had a bottle in my hand under the table all the time he was talking & anyway Lang stopped him. Not because Lang likes me any more than Martin but a couple people came in while we were sitting there and the joint use to have a reputaton for 3 shootings they had there a couple years ago and Lang was told to keep his nose clean by the cops if he wanted to operate in that neighborhood as they did not want more complaints. "Oh well he is not worth brusing my knuckles on" said Martin and I laughed in his face and he went out.

Well Martin has something on Lang o.k. because I found out from the cashier that Herta is getting 50 now. The nerve of this Martin, he still brings his wife to the joint and Herta often goes & sits with Mrs. M. and she is old enough to be her mother, so I guess it is one of those things where a woman would rather have her husband chasing around after young girls just as long as he don't get a divorce. You cant tell me any different. I see it all too clear why I could not move in on Herta. These "innocent" ones are the ones alright. If I was a little more innocent maybe I would be right up there getting 2 grand a wk. etc.

Well Ted, give my love to everybody in 802 except

about 5000 heels that all think that all they need is just a little 8 piece combinaton and they would have the best little band etc. etc. Drop me a line but be careful who you give my address to.

PAL JOEY

Joey on the Cake Line

FRIEND TED:

Well Xmas is coming and the geese are getting fat,
please put a penny in the blind man's hat as the old
saying use to go but not that I am asking you to put a
penny in my hat or am not a blind man either as far
as that is concerned. I never saw the day wherein
no matter how much moola I had I could not use
some more but I am saving you for a big touch in case
I want to start my own band in competition with you
(who knows I may be kidding on the level and that
would be quite irony if it ever happened?) I do not
know why it is that I sound like everything was sharp
and I was right up there because if you want the
truth and the whole truth and nothing but the truth
you pal Joey is on the cake line. That is my way of
putting it that I am on the bread line only I am still a
little better off. You get what I have reference to
about cake & bread. It was a famous historical topper
when Josephine, the wife of Napoleon was informed
that the poor people did not have any bread to eat
and she said "Why dont they eat some cake if they
havent any bread." Very good considering what they
did was lop off her conk for saying it. Well I got my
head lopped off too but not for making any crack. I
went to the club one nite to give with the vocal chorus

and add some class to the joint with my new midnite
blue tails only there was no club there. That is the
place was burn to the ground. 10,000 nite clubs in this
country but I guessed they repealed the law of aver-
ages because they had to pick the one I was in to
have a fire. I noticed I never get that kind of odds
when I go to the track. But who is complaning. I
know one lug is complaning but will come to him
later. So this nite I went there and all there was was
ropes and fire hoses with ice hanging down and the
joint stank worse than ever because you burn some
rugs and pour some water on it and the water freezes
to ice and you have some stink. Believe you me. Well
there was nobody around but some firemen and a cop
I know and the cop pointed to the joint and said to
me "The hottest nite spot in Chicago" and I asked
him what caused it and he said kiddingly "I guess
some sparks from your singing." I have enough on
him to crucify him but he lets me park anywhere so
I did not report him. It seems I did not read the afternoon papers when I got up that afternoon and did
not know there was this fire. Well I finally got in
touch with the "owners" and they said act of God and
fire etc. wash up a contract automatically and I said
to them to wait a minute I did not have a contract. I
didnt either and I did not want them babies to think
they had me under contract because another spot was
making me offers but they did not understand what
I meant but tho't I was going to try to hold them up
for my week as it was only a Tues. So they said "Joey
you are the 1st one to come here and did not try to
make some trouble for us and with us you are a right
guy altho it is a pleasant surprise, ever if we would of
had a contract we would not had to pay you because
of fire and act of God but let us repeat you are a right

guy and any time we open up again we hire you before we even hire a waiter." So I saw what they were thinking I meant when I said I did not have a contract. They were thinking I was giving them a break so I said "Well what the hell, I said. I do not pretend I am some kind of a patsy but you fellows always put it on the line for me every pay day and gave me good billing so I did not want to come here only to offer you my sympathy and if I had some moola put away I would even lend you some or any part of it to open up again." One of them looked at the other and looked at me and then at the other and said "Well, I have seen everything" and then he stood up and shook hands and said "As you know we are only the front men here as the backers do not wish to appear but as long as we are in this business one guy will always have a job and it is you Joey. How are you fixed?" So I said well you saw that new midnite blue tailcoat I just bo't I said that was not paid for only partly, just the down payment. I said you know how it is in this business a guy has to have a front and I would hate to lose that and they realized it and said they would give me my week right away and reached in his pocket and pealed off 5 20s, my week. I tho't I might as well give it to them but good so I said not if they couldnt spare it and they said that was alright. Then Solly the one fellow said he had been thinking it over and he had a little propositon for me and it was this. He said for me to keep going around to the good spots every nite and make contacts until they opened up again and then when they did I would still be a big attracton because people would not get the chance to forget me and get myself some publicity as much as possible and he would leave that to me. I started to say what would I use for moola and he said to me "I anticipate yr. queston. We in this business hate each others guts but we all have to co-operate with one another and all I have to do is call the boys that run the other joints and tell them I would apprisiate it providing they would not slap a couvert on you and I personally will give you 50 a wk to pay yr expenses, how does that look to you?" Well you know how it look to me. Getting paid for what I would do anyway so I shook on it and so that is what I am doing and do not have to worry about another job but am ruining the vocal chords smoking too much in joints and only singing once in a while when some m.c. says "I see we have another celebrity in our mist" and introduces me and I give. So that is why I am on the cake line not the bread line.

But will have to tell you a funny story like I hinted above regarding one fellow that is complaning. I did menton how I bo't this tailor-made tailcoat but only pd. the down payment. It is midnite blue and it fits me like a sword holder fits a sword. About a wk. before the joint burned down I got delivery on this tailcoat and had to con the tailor into letting me have it for only the down payment. All told it was to cost me $100. I put down 25 down payment. But I said to him how can I pay you if you dont leave me wear it and I lose my job. So when they had the fire I went to him and said he could have it back as I could not pay for it and he yelled bloody murder and I walked out on him and said go ahead sue because you cannot garnishy my salary as I have no salary and anyway I am bankrupted. Im not but how does he know. So he had to take it back then I got a guy in the band with the same build I have and he went in to the same fellow and said he was thinking of having a tails made and the tailor did not know it was a friend of mine and he said "I have just the thing for you. A customer did not call for this" proving he was a crook. My pal said well he wanted one more conservative not blue but the tailor said "I will tell you what I will do I will let you have it for $65 the latest thing." My friend said he was not thinking of paying that kind of money and anyway he could get a ready made for 40. So the tailor came down to 45 and my pal said okay. He took it. So I gave my pal a fin for his acting ability and so all told I got my tailcoat for a total of 75. They always overcharge you anyway those tailors because they figure on losing dough when they give credit and bad debts etc. So I just paid him what the damn thing was worth altho on me it is very becoming as they say in that gag.

I guess you got my Xmas card. A funny thing. I ordered two kinds this Xmas, the kind I sent you and also the conservative ones with very formal Greetings of the Season and a stage coach & four and my name engraved on it. They were for the Onawentsia crowd friends but "accidentally" I got one of the ones I sent you in the envelope with the stage coach ones and now I understand the whole town is talking about the amusing cards. Everybody wanted to know who posed for it. Nobody did as the fellow that drew it copied it out of *Esquire* but I just look wise when anybody says they think it was so and so or this one or that. It certanly got me plenty publicity.

Well Merry Christmas, as the saying goes. Guess I will have to go to bed for 24 hrs so I dont have to stop hating my fellow men. But that does not go for you, Ted. The best.

PAL JOEY

The Erloff

FRIEND TED:

In my prevous communicaton I informed you how I guess it was some critic of singing set fire to the joint I was singing in and I was out of a job. I am only kidding about the place being set fire by a music critic because what I hear the singing in Chicago does not have any high standards to acheive (sneeze when you say that Pal). They tell me it is been going on for years but I only just heard about the singers here, how what you do is get some guy that his idea of music is when he heard them sticking the little pigs in their throat down at the stock yards, which is plenty loud and plenty high (especially high at the stock yards if you get what I referring to and hold yr. nose at that gag). That is their idea of music and the 1st thing you know they are knocking themselves out indevouring to sign some baby that sings loud and high and sign her up to sing opera. At but all the moola a week anybody can spend not excepting I. Had I but known of this at an earlier age I would of made the nessary preparatons and arrangements and wd. be a soprano now at plenty moola a wk. instead of being somewhere between Frankie Parker outdoors on a rainy nite and the Groaner giving an imitation of a cry of joy or scared of a mouse.

I told you I had this deal with my ex-boss, 50 a wk
to go around the other joints and make an appearance so the public wd not forget me until my boss
opened up again. Well I had this little mouse, a very
nice little spivot that belong to the college crowd at
the Northwestern U. I think you played a job there
two yrs ago at a "prom" so you know about it. They
have some nice mice out there and she was one. I had
her out this nite and over came a chap I say hello to
occasonally, and he is a member of the Saddle &
Cycle Club. Alright I am kidding you and this is
1939 or 1940 (I have not got it straight yet) and they
do not have any club name the Saddle & Cycle only
they do!!! 1940! Anyway this is a rich playboy type of
a chap and kind of an Ed. Arnold type. He does all
the talking so I do not have to tell him any lies and
when he saw me and this mouse he said to join him
as they are going slumming. Slumming was what he
said and slumming was what he meant. From one of
the top rooms in Chi we go bang to a joint that is a
joint. The mouse with me is strictly no cigar and the
daughter of a small town banker in Indiana and have
a summer home up in Mich. and I am thinking of
next summer when I take her out. So she is not the
one I would of pick to go with me to a joint like the
one we went. But she said she wanted to go and when
I said yes her guess was as good as mine where we
were heading. Strictly a bruhaha. But Sat. nite! This
guy that took us is well known or else I would of
turned around the minute we got there. In we go.
Wide open like a movie of a mining camp town. An
ugly old hag of an Irish lady is yelling for help altho
using the words of I Want the Waiter with the Water
and accompanied by maybe her uncle or maybe her
son, a man that should of been in bed hrs ago. I am

not kidding. He thumped out the bass and drank his beer at the same time and it was not on purpose. I mean it was not a gay 90 gag. They were leveling. So pretty soon our party got seated at our table and this little old guy came over and I tho't here is an old guy and in a minute he is going to take out a piece of rope and ask the gentlemen to tie him up and inside of 2 mins. he will be free. That was what he looked like. But when he came over to our table Preston stood up and shook hands with him and introduced everybody to him and told him to sit down which he did. Well his name was Paddy Dunlin and all he is is the owner of the joint. Not only of this particular joint but about 50 other ones. I do not wish to get ahead of my story but in plain words the old corpse has girls anywhere from two bits to whatever you want to pay for. And the face of a saint as they say. Anyway he sat down next to me and had a beer on Preston and when the other members of our party got up to dance, he looked me over and then he whispered to me "What about the erloff." I said what a couple times. I finally caught on that he was asking me what about the little mouse. Oh, nothing, I said. "Slumming" he said. Then he said "What do you think of the erloff" and this time I did not say what but watched him. He made a gesture with his head and his expresson and that meant he was asking me what did I think of the joint. I stalled to think of something and he had to go away to answer the phone and Preston came back to the table and gave me some facts on the old guy. He said I was not in Chi long enough to know about him. He said the old guy was over 70 and was running joints from the time he was 21 yrs of age. There was a story around that when they had that bank holiday one of the railroad cos had to come to the old guy for cash. He had over 2 million in cash. Hotels, railroads, all the respectable big cos had to come to him for cash. He said (Preston) how for yrs every morning the sisters came around and collected choice meats like steaks & chops etc. that was left over from the nite before, and took it away and gave it to the poor. Also potatoes and salad and red beets etc. Also butter and bread. The works. Every single morning. He was always good for a roof on a church just as long as it was Catholic. He buried thousands of people that would of been buried in the potter's field if he did not get up the dough. Charity after charity. But then they gave an order that nobody was to take any more from the old guy. It made him sad and he almost began hitting the sauce, but his elderly wife would not allow him in the house with booze on his breath so he just did not drink.

I listened attentively because Preston was paying for the party but if you want the truth I was bore to death with Preston and with his old charachter. That was what Preston called him a fascinating old charachter. To me he was a dirty old man with a lot of moola. I was even thinking rapid calculation how much it would cost to take my little mouse out to her sororty house by taxi instead of waiting till Preston decided to take us home and just then the old man returned from his phone call. He must of got a big order from some Amer. Leg. conventon because he was smiling when he sat down with us.

The old dame got up again and began horsewhipping The Lamp is Low. Dunlin said to me "How do you like the erloff" and I said fine. Great I said. "Right" he said. "She is been with me fifteen yrs." And I thought to myself yes and you must of looked her over a long long time before hiring her too. Her

and the band been with me 15 yrs he said. I said that
was wonderful these days to have such loyalty going
on but to myself I tho't yes you all stick together to
keep warm like old cows out on the range during a
blizzard. I had a look at the band. He had them hid
behind some palms but there was one old guy playing
cornet that looked as if he was worried for fear that
the Confederates wd catch him for being a deserter.
"The erloff, they like the erloff" said Dunlin. Everything was erloff with this decrept old bore and I was
thinking to myself 2 million cash or no 2 million cash,
old man or no old man, he is driving me nuts so I am
going to break a 5 dollar bill over some hack driver's
head and take my little mouse home in a taxi but I
am glad I didn't because just then the old man says
to me "Of course in the Loop you got a different
erloff Joey." I said what? "The erloff, he said. They
like noise here and that's the way I like it. You
would just as well come wearing a shell if you ever
took a job in a spot like this, that is how big an egg
you would lay. But the class people that go to the
rooms you been working in like hardly any noise at
all." Well he called me Joey and I was figuring all the
while he tho't I was a Cycle Club boy but no. He
made me the minute he saw me, as the detectives
say. He said he understood I was a sock the last 2
rooms I worked and right out in front of the little
mouse he said 100 a wk was not enough for a handsome chap that could put over a ballad and have the
women with their tongue hanging out. "Don't worry,
he said when you open up again you will be getting
one five o. You also have a nice personality for that
kind of a room." I said I certanly would appprisiate
him giving me a plug with the owners and he looked
at me and said "Are you kidding? *I* own that joint."

Then he got up and walked away and I was too surprised to think for a minute and tho't I plumbered it but we have opened up again in another room and I am getting one five o. The erloff Pal.

Always your
PAL JOEY

Even the Greeks

FRIEND TED:

I don't think I will be able to take it out here much more. In the 1st place it is because you never saw cold weather until you spent a winter in Chi. I do not mean weather like you have to chop the alcohol before putting it in the radator of the car. I mean weather that is so cold that the other day this pan handler came up to me and braced me and said I look as if I had a warm heart and I gave him a two-bit piece because if it wasnt for him would not of known I was alive or frozen to death. That has how it has been here in Chi. Maybe that explains some of the pecular actons of many of the inhabitants. Illinois is a state of suspended animaton and the people live in hibernaton from Oct. to whenever it ever gets warmer. I do not know and hope I am not here long enough to find out. I am merely telling you this in case you ever decide to take a job to spend the winter in Chi and I am not there to stop you at the point of a gun.

Well if you think I am trying to infer that I have been running up against some of the pecularities of the local natives you will only be 100% correct. The club opened up again after the fire as you no doubt read here or there like in the *Variety* or the *Down*

Beat. We got off to good business but that was to be
expect it. It wd of surprised me had it been otherwise
so only menton it in passing. What I want to tell you
is about the pecular local people and this one case.
Two wacks if ever I saw one and they are Nick the
prop. of the Olympia rest. and Pete that works for
him in the kitchen. The Olympia is on my way home
when I am on my way home if you know what I
mean.

I just as soon never go home but a man has to
have his rest so when I go home ever since I have
been living where I now am I use to stop in at the
Olymp. for a coffee and raison cake before going to
bed. I got to be a regular customer there and Nick
would expect me to come in around 3, 4 in the morning so as to relive the monotony with a wise crack or
two and I guess Nick was very grateful to me because
one nite I heard somebody out in the kitchen yell
"right" and a minute or two later out through the hole
in the wall bet. kitchen and rest. a plate slid and on
the plate was some food. Nick was just about going
to throw it in the garbage and then he noticed me and
he said "could you use a ham omlet?" I said sure. So
he gave me the ham omlet, or what ever it was. I
asked him what was wrong with it but he said nothing
was wrong and go ahead and eat it if I preferred to.
So I ate it and it was as good a ham omlet as I ever
ate.

A nite or so after I went in Nick's again and was
having a cup of coffee and once more I heard somebody out in the kitchen yell "right" and a couple
minutes later out came a jelly omlet and once more
Nick looked at me and said could I eat a jelly omlet
and I said I could force one and he assured me that
there was nothing phony about it but go ahead and

eat it and it was as good a jelly omlet as any jelly omlet I ever ate.

Then I went in the next nite and ordered a coffee and waited but Nick didn't offer me anything. Then the nite after that I went in and sure enough some-body out in the kitchen yelled "right" and in a minute or so out came a beautiful club sandwich. Nick asked me again could I use a club sandwich and I said I tho't maybe I could and it was a tasty club sandwich which I enjoyed to the hilt. So that was the way it went. Some nites hungry and not wishing to throw away a dollar I wd go to Nick's hoping to get an om-let or tasty sandwich but no cigar. I wd not get a thing. Other nites I wd go in and get like a small steak one nite. But I began to notice one thing. The only times I got a free meal it was when the fellow out in the kitchen suddenly yelled out "right." No-body wd order anything but he wd yell it and then in a minute or two something very tasty wd come through the opening. So naturally I wd wait around hoping this fellow in the kitchen wd yell "right" be-cause if he did that meant I wd get a free meal. So all the time naturally I was helping Nick relive the mo-notony by chatting about this and that and one night the usual thing. The fellow yelled, out came liver & bacon and Nick just looked at me and at the liver and bacon and I said sure. Then my curosity got the better of me and I asked him. I said "Nick what's with the free food? Explain." So he said eat my liver and bacon and he wd explain the entire mystery. So I ate it and then he said to look out in the kitchen and I wd see a husky well built man about 50 yrs of age sweeping up or polishing pots and pans. That is Pete, said Nick. "Pete use to be the best short order cook I ever ran across in all my experience in this business. But one

day Pete's wife ran away with a wrestler and took
their three little ones with them and Pete began hitting the sauce and got into a fight and somebody hit
him over the conk with a bung starter and he was
never the same after that. But Nick knew Pete as boys
in the old country and Nick made up his mind that
Pete wd always have a job as long as he owned a rest.
So Nick had to hire another cook and gave Pete
the job sweeping up. But every once in a while while
sweeping up Pete wd think he heard Nick order
something like a ham omlet or small steak or one of
the other dishes that Pete was good at and he wd put
down his broom and go and cook the omlet or whatever he tho't he heard. Oh and I forgot to say in there
that when he wd think he wd hear Nick ordering he
wd yell out "right" and then start cooking it. I said to
Nick that must run into money. Yes, it does, said Nick
but that is okay and anyway you are here to eat the
stuff so I do not have to throw it away.

Well that is all about Nick and Pete and I do not
know which one is wackiest either Nick for keeping
Pete or Pete himself. You can make up your mind as
I have my own idea. But that is the way they are in
this town. Even the Greeks.

Your
PAL JOEY

Joey and the Calcutta Club

PAL TED:

Well, Chum, the poor man's Bing Crosby is still making with the throat here in Chi. but if the present good fortune keeps up I ought to be getting the New York break pretty soon. The trouble is up to now the good fortune has been keeping so far up it is up in the stratuspere out of sight. But never out of mind, kiddy. Never out of mind. N.Y. is where I belong N.Y. or Hollywood or will settle for both. However have been off the bread line and working steady but you do not see me on the caviare line yet and was always a one to have the ambiton to starve to death within reach of caviare if you get what I mean. If I have to starve to death it would be this way, namely, have about 5 lbs. of caviare and filet mignon & champagne etc. but me too God damn lazy to reach for it. Maybe to make it perfect I would be firsting my attentons on like Hedy La Marr instead of just plain lazy and would be so busy would forget to eat. That is the manner in which I would prefer to starve to death.

Well, speaking of the charming opposite sex I have a little spot of annecdotes (I dote on annecdotes) to tell you which may amuse the chappies around Lebuses and give them all my best excepting those that I would not say I would not spit on them as I can

hardly wait to spit on them. Well this is the story and
not only a story but also a good thing to keep in mind
in case you get in the same situaton some time yourself.

Shortly after I got started working here, a little
mouse came in one nite with a party of six and naturally began asking for request nos. and in that way
I got aquainted and also thru knowing one of the guys
on the party. It was not a spending party, strictly
cufferoo. The guy is a fellow named Quinn on one of
the local papers here in Chi. and covers nite clubs,
etc. and signs his initials L. Q. to reviews he gives the
spots here & there but mostly in the Loop etc. So
Quinn asked me to join them and I did and this
mouse with them named Jean Benedict looks like
10000 other dames on the line of some Bway show
except when she opens her trap she has an accent
that is so British even Sir Nevile Chamberlin would
not be able to understand her. I knew she was strictly
U.S.A. by appearance but the accent is so good I think
what is the angle. What gives, I asked her, altho not
in so many words. I inquired how she happen to have
the accent and she said a lot of people inquire of her
the same thing and it is easily explained. She is half
American and her father is British. Well she sounded
so refined I wanted to say a few one syllable words to
her to note the effect to see if she would know what I
meant. Well I did not, not that nite. About three
nites later. The 1st nite all she did was say why didn't
I call her up at her flat and drop in for a gin and "it."
I said the "it" was o. k. with me if we were both talking about the same thing and she put on the act as
if not getting "it" and then said priceless. Oh, how
wrong she was when she said priceless but am getting ahead of my story.

Well on acc't of a certan other obligaton which I
mentoned in my previous letter I could not give my
full attenton to Miss Benedict but will just say in passing if I would of given her any more attenton at the
rate I was going I would now not be cutting paper
dolls. Oh no. I would not be able to lift a paper doll.
However let me suffice it to say that I moved in &
during the course of our more dull conversatons I
accertain that Miss Benedict is living with this other
mouse whom I do not meet. They are sharing this
flat. Also she tells me her dear mother and dear papa
are in dear old London. I never asked her that. All
I asked her was did she live alone, etc. and now I recall it she certanly did jump at the chance to explain
about the old man and the mother. I should of known
that the English have more reserve about personal
affairs but I guess I had good reason to forget all
about reserve in connecton with Miss B. Anyway she
gave me the routine about father & mother being in
London that day and two days later when "love
dropped in for tea" meaning me, she kept standing by
the window and looking out and when I would say
anything to her she would act like as if she did not
hear me and then I finally said pardon me but remember me I am yr. pal Joey, the fellow that just
came in about 15 mins. ago and didnt we meet at
the club etc. She said "I apologize" but she was upset
and maybe it would be better if I did not stay but
went out to a picture that day as she was not herself.
I must say the girl is an actress because I honestly
tho't I squeezed it out of her that her check from her
old man was late and she said no doubt because of
the way things have been in dear old London. She
said she always got her check of $300 by the 7th of
the month, sometimes earlier depending on how soon

the boats arrived from London. But here it was the 10 or 11 of the month and no check and no letter either. The check always came with a letter and she worried about if they sent her father off on some misson for the gov't and it was so important he was not allowed to leave her know he was even going away. He was some important fellow in the office that runs India and maybe they sent him there. It was not only the money but what if it was an important dangerous misson? What about her mother, I inquired? Well, she said that was where she swore me to secrecy and told me that her mother was an American but also had a lot to do with India, also some kind of an agent but American in name only so as to keep her passport. Well of course all this went on for a half an hr. and eventually I was a sucker for the touch. I admit it. I let her have $75.

Well I gave her my oath I would not tell about her people being sort of spies against India but even so would not of told anybody about it as I did not want it to get around that I went for a $75 touch as you get the reputaton of being a soft touch like that and pretty soon girls from all over the country are waiting at yr. dressing room and also I had this "other obligaton" if *she* heard I was putting out 75 here and there she would take back her car and maybe even get me the bounceroo from this spot. So I kept quite but one nite soon after I happen to see Quinn and went over to thank him for a nice menton and he started out by asking me how was Miss Benedict. I played dumb and he said, "Oh, I tho't you were in. I took for granted you were in and how did you happen to miss that as I was given to understand that you are a young man that moved right in." Well imagine. I burned and said "Listen, wise guy not only am I in but the nite you bro't her here she slipped me her phone no. with you sitting at the table." I could of cut my throat when I realized what I said, insulting the guy after he gave me the good notice but instead he did not get sore. On the contrary he replied, "Ah, then perhaps you will join our little club. What did she take you for?" I said for nothing. And he said "Oh, you can level with me, do you mean to say she did not put the touch on you for a little, like a yard?" So I admitted it and then he told me. It seems that I was a member of quite a club, and a paid up member too. Miss B. took Quinn for 50 and another guy for 50 and another for 75 and one guy for around 300, a middle aged fellow that sold religous articles to churches and did not want any trouble. So Quinn said we ought to form a club called the Calcutta Club after the town over in India. Well I saw the humor of it but I would of liked to give Miss B. a kick in the stomach if she came along at the time.

Well I put it down to experence and tho't no more of it till about two wks. later Quinn came in and told me he had a propositon, not his but Miss B's. It seems what she did was take our India money and move out and get a more expensive flat by herself without the girl friend and after she moved in she was there about two weeks and met some guy from Milwaukee that tho't she was right and so much so that this guy was already talking wedding bells even before he moved in. She had him thinking it made her sick to see a woman smoke and she never went out to nite spots but always had a good book around. How she picked him up I don't know but he was going for everything. He had no suspicons aroused because at the time she was absolutely staying away from the spots. Well she only had two wks. to go she told Quinn be-

fore the rent was due and that meant only two wks.
to work on the prospect from Milwaukee, so the
propositon she put to Quinn was if we would stake
her to the next month's rent and she felt sure that was
all she would need. He asked me what I tho't of it and
he said frankly he had no $50 to throw away but he
would rather throw the 50 away on a chance of getting the 100 back and he advised me to do the same.
He won me over but I told him on one conditon,
namely, how did we know there was this sucker from
Milwaukee and so it was agreed that if she could pro-
duce him and convince us then we would put up the
ready. So that was how it was and a nite or two later
she came in the club and him with her and I took one
quick gander at and was convinced but to make sure
I stopped at the table suddenly like I just recognized
him and said, "I beg yr. pardon but havent we met.
I am sure I met you in Milwaukee last yr." and the
way he got red and said no I knew he was from Milwaukee and I also knew something Miss B. did not
know as smart as she was, namely, he was dumb but
not that dumb that he would marry her, but was willing to put up the rent etc. Well that was o.k. She pretend to go to the little girls rm. and I had a talk
with her and told her I was in favor of the propositon
and would tell the other members of the club I was
and she would have the front money. But I also told
her that Mr. Milwaukee was not going to marry her
if I knew human nature and she said to me, "Joey,
darling, I could almost like you for being so intelligent, if for nothing else." She said "I told Quinn that
Chubby (the nickname for the Milwaukee guy) did
not move in but he did move in but Quinn is a dope
and I had to tell him a good story. What I want the
front money for is so Chubby will get expensive ideas

and not get the idea that he is only going for coffee
and cakes dough." Then she gave me a little kiss on
the cheek and said "that will have to be all for the
present but we shall see what we shall see." So the
boys all got their dough back last wk. including me
but I got mine in three 50 dollar bills inclosed in a
gold clip with a watch on it. You have to admire a girl
like that from Buffalo, N.Y. where she is from. That is
how English she is. She has relatons in Canada. Anyway she is a very smart little operator and I predict
great things for her. She got me putting on a little wt.
as Chubby likes caviare and she always keeps some in
the frigidair for him but all we singers put on wt. like
Caruso, McCormick, Crosby, etc.

Yrs.
PAL JOEY

Joey and Mavis

FRIEND TED:

I do not wish this to constitute a regular letter as am only setting down my tho'ts at random more or less as they come to me sitting here casually after dinner while Mavis is at the movies with the kids. Perhaps a few words about Mavis would not be a miss as I have had so many things happening to me since writing you before that I did not get the opportunity to inform you regarding Mavis who has bro't such changes into my life that I can not believe it myself when I stop to think of it.

It happened one nite (from the picture of the same name) and I just finished a set and was outside on the sidewalk in front of the joint filling up my lungs with Gods air & some of my own cigarette smoke instead of 50 other people's and was talking to the doorman Sailor Bob a punchy stumble-bum that after 20 yrs learned how to open the door of that new inventon the auto but did not catch on how to close it. I use to go out and stand there & leave him pay me a few compliments on my voice as he tho't himself a great hand as a singer. He could not of been a worse fighter than a singer otherwise he would of been worm meat 20 yrs ago or more and none of this would of happened. He appprisiated my singing I will say

that for him altho always asking why didnt I sing like
Oh you beautiful doll which you are too young to remember and so am I but the story I hear is that when
the Titantic went down (a ship) people sang it or
hummed a couple bars and then said the hell with this
and jumped the hell off the boat so they would not
have to finish singing it. I do not know that for sure
but only base that on hearsay based on a weak moment when I allowed the Sailor to sing it for me one
nite. I tho't why does this happen to me, everything
happens to me. I tho't I was the poor man's good
Samaratan to listen to that but was glad later as one
nite I was on on my way out and some guy that had
suspicons of me & his wife was waiting for me and I
was doing some very fast talking when out of the
corner of my eye I saw the Sailor and yelled to him
and I must say that what the Sailor can not do with
his fist he does not have to do as he does it with the
boot. I have seen some dirty fighting in my travels
with the socialites and polo players I grew up with
but nothing to compare with the Sailor who is a pleasure to watch work if you care for that sort of thing
and I do especially when he is working on somebody
that a minute ago was going to stick their fist down
my throat. Anyway the guy had the wrong party as it
was not me but the drummer in the band. I had her
sister and it was not even the right nite he was referring to.

Well as I started in to say this one nite I went out
and the Sailor was on duty and I was more less fronting for him, that is on smoking. He was not allow to
smoke on duty but it was o. k. for me to so I would
say "I will light one for you Sailor" and if the mgr.
came out the Sailor would hand it to me and would
not get caught smoking on duty. Then this 1937 La

Salle sedan came up and four got out, two couples.
The fellow driving asked if it would be o.k. to park
here and the Sailor working for a tip stalled and said
not as a rule but in this case etc. so the fellow driving
gave him a buck and they went inside. I do not know
how I happen to miss Mavis but I did not see her until I had to go in again and polish off some more dittys
and they had a table ringside, and I went over and
asked them if they had any request nos. and Mavis
asked for two requests but did not have both of them
only the Beguin no. The other was an oldy like My
Buddy which they were singing during the civil war.
I know it but forgot the lyrics. She looked around 32
or 33, inclined to take on a little weight but I also
like them zoftick as some goose in the band says.
They asked me to sit down with them and join them
in a drink but I could not have a drink on the job but
we got into conversaton and in the course of the conversaton she happen to menton that when she saw me
outside talking to the doorman she tho't perhaps I
was there waiting for a date instead of working in the
joint and she meant it as a compliment as she said
this spot was new to her and she did not like to go to
strange spots but thinking I was the type customer
the joint got she figured it was o. k. I said I considered
her a very wise person and I was not kidding because all the time I kept looking at her I kept adding
up how much she had on her was worth. At least a
two-caret diamond ring on the engagement finger and
also a diamond bracelet and a gold cigarette case with
inside it (not outside) her three initials in diamonds
M. W. K. (for Mavis Williams Ketchell but did not
find that out till later). The people with her were in
their 40s. Well I always make it a point to leave a
table while they still want me to stay (always leave

them laughing) so I moved away and merely said I
hope they would come again etc. I could not figure
out any way how to get her phone no. without asking for one on the chin. I had some preminiton that
I could move in if I played it right but was also not
sure. I could not figure if maybe one of the two guys
bo't those diamonds or if she had her own dough or if
she was a wealthy young divorcee or young widow
or what the hell? She was so cagey that all I knew
about her was all she wanted to let me know. Even
so I had that preminiton that once I got alone with
her I would let her do the talking and maybe she
would talk herself into it.

Well I went out again for a smoke and of course
asked the Sailor who own the La Salle but he never
saw it before and I could not get any clue but just
then fate fell into my hands. At first I tho't my luck
ran out because here they were all coming out, Mavis
& the other three. The one fellow backed up the sedan
and the others got in and then when they were all in
the other dame decided she wanted to sit in back
with "Harry" and Mavis got out and the other dame
got in the back and sat with Harry and Mavis started
to get in front with the other guy and just when she
was sitting down the Sailor must of decided that the
important thing was on the seat because just then he
slammed the door and got her right foot. She let out
one "Jesus H. Christ" and then I saw her face and she
was biting her lower lip in pain. Trying to keep from
crying I guess but very couragous. Then when she
had a look at her foot she passed out and I damn near
did too. The Sailor put everything in that slam and it
would take your appetite away to describe her foot. I
saw it all happen.

Well plenty of excitement. The mgr. came out and

the Sailor was non compass mentis and did not know
what to do and the other dame was screaming like she
was the one that had the door slammed on her own
foot instead of Mavis. They finally got a dr. and they
took Mavis to a hospital. One of the guys in the car
took my name etc. and all I could think of was that
fixed it fine as far as Mavis coming back to the joint
for a while or maybe ever. The way her foot looked it
would be lucky if she did not lose the foot. But it was
not as bad as I tho't and a day or two later a guy came
around to my place and asked me a lot of questons
about how it happened. He was from the ins. co. he
said and I tho't he meant the ins. co. that Mavis was
insured by but no, he was from the one that covered
the joint for accidents like that. I told him a story that
should of got Mavis $1,000,000. The next wk. I got the
bounceroo from the joint. It seems that they settled
with Mavis for around $1100 but if I would of had a
different story ready maybe they could of got away
without settling for anything. I still dont know all the
angles and do not give a damn. I told the mgr. if I
knew what kind of a story he wanted me to tell maybe I would of told a different one but he said it was
just too bad they did settle. I was out and also the
Sailor.

But I guess the Sailor can always get himself a spot
in some gym but there I was with only about $85 in
my poke and no job. So I was desperate and almost
wired you to put the touch on you but at the last moment got this idea and decided to call on Mavis at
the hosp. I did so and much to my pleasant surprise was told to go right up to room whatever it was.
She was surrounded with flowers and was glad to see
me instead of giving me the brush which was what I
was afraid of. She had her foot in a plaster cast and

first she made me feel at home and then said for me
to take a pencil and write my name on the cast as she
understood I saw the whole thing and must of told the
truth about how it happened otherwise they would
not of settled so quickly. "Yes," I said. "I was too
truthful for my own good, Mrs. Ketchell, as they discharged me because I was ready to go to court and
tell the truth that the doorman was to blame for the
unfortunate accident." She tho't a minute and said
she wished she knew that at the time before settling,
however she asked me to sign my autograph on the
cast and I did.

Well we chatted and she asked me to come and
see her again and I said I would be happy to as I
would have plenty of time and she said that was perfect because most of her friends worked in the day
time and she did not have many woman friends in
Chicago that could come and call on her and it was
such a bore in the hospital alone. So I started going
there every day and soon she told me the story of her
life and how she was so happy with her two children
and husband but one day he came home and shot
himself and the ins. co. had to pay double because
that was in the clause and she could not bear to
live in the small town where her home was because it
was too full of memories so she came to Chi. Her husband was 20 yrs. older than she and she was hardly
more than a girl when she got married but even so
was happy with him as he did every thing in the
world for her. Well I can tell you one thing in the
world he did not do for her because I am no 20 years
older than she is and no old guy 50-some years old did
everything in the world for her. They could attach a
wire to her and I bet she could light up a city of
50,000 populaton the way they did with some ship out

on the Coast. After she got out of the hospital she got
me to take a room near where she has an apartment
for herself & the two kids. She knows a guy that is going to back a new joint in the Loop dist. and when the
thing is ready I am practically set to open there and
meanwhile we go out about every nite. I caught her
in a few lies but this is on the level and I think she has
something on the guy that is backing the new spot as
one nite we were on our way in a place and he was
standing there waiting and she said to him, "How
nice to see you, Tom" and introduced me and said I
was just the singer for the new spot and he began to
stall and she said not to bore her but just make an
appointment with me and he said "Oh, is it that
way?" and she replied "Why, Tom darling, just what
do you mean?" and laughed and he said o.k. and I see
him next Tues. I sure would hate to let her get anything on me.

Well she ought to be back soon and I want to put
this in the envelope and seal it up and when she
sees I was writing to a guy and not some dame it
should make her a happy girl. Age 37 if I can believe her drivers license.

I wonder what the poor people are doing?

Regards
PAL JOEY

A New Career

FRIEND TED:

By the business we are doing these nites one wd never be let to suspect that there is a world conflagraton going on but nevertheless such is the case. The rope is up every nite of the wk except Monday and then such is the kind of lug I am working for that he wants to put the rope up and hang himself from it because one nite of the wk maybe four tables do not get occupied by people buying wine. This is the same guy that I recall distintly six months ago if 4 tables did happen to be occupied he wd spend $40 phoning his girl on the road with some band that business was terrific. Now when he gets a bad nite he thinks it is brutal.

I guess you are wondering why I am giving you these physical details. Well I do not blame you because why should you give a good God damn about some crib in Chicago even if I do happen to be working there. Of course I always give a damn if it is you and I understand you are going to be booked into the N.Y. Paramount in a couple wks and whoever's record is tops I hope you break it and am sure you will. But of course why you should care if we do 8000 or 800 except that I have a little propositon that may arouse yr interest and it is this.

I will tell you all about it and how I happen to have my interest aroused. It is owing to those Monday nites. My boss is known by the name Harry Bonbon which is a mob nickname he got from the mobsters not because of him liking chocolate bon-bon candy but his name was Burnbaum and they had a mobster with an impedima in his speech and the closest he could come to the name was Bonbon. That is one ver- tion. However that is an good as any and I just wanted to tell you his name Harry Bonbon. So these Monday nites he just sits there chewing on the end of his cigar (personally I wish he would chew on the lit end but no such luck) and he counts the empties and then I see him looking around and he will call a headwaiter and point to some lights and say "Save that" and the headwaiter will have to go out and turn off the light. He keeps doing that until by the time it gets to be 12 or half past the place is like a black out over France. It is a very handy thing for the out of town spenders that have some local mouse out for the first time and want to find out if she has a wooden leg. It also is a very fine thing in favor of the light finger gentery and I told Harry one Monday I said in case he was interested over there was a bump man I use to see out at the track some times and I said maybe he is now working alone but it will be a fine thing for the joint in case he happens to bump in- to one of the socialites and the socialites lose a hand- some wallet stuffed with a liberal supply of folding. "Jesus! said Harry, I never tho't of that and or- dered the lights turned on. Of course he has only been in this business since around 1885 and should know by this time that any time the socialites go out they leave there folding money at home or most of it. My experence with socialites is they go to a spot with the expectaton of throwing away up to $3 if it is a party of 2 or 4.

Well that is just an illustration of what I mean about Monday nite and how Harry worries. If it is not the lights it is go easy on the ice or use napkins instead of fresh table clothes. Or go easy on the air conditoning or no fresh packs of matches but use the old packs with one match in them or else he is got the cashier going nuts because he wants a report every 15 min. So of course I also noticed another thing more important than the above. I happen to notice him one nite looking at me. He did not say anything. He merely looked. But the way he looked was the way the head man looks on one of those artic expeditons after nobody had anything to eat for a wk. They are going around barefooted because they have used up their moccassins for scoff. Maybe one of the chaps has knawed off a nice juicey thumb. But the head man is looking at me. I am the fat one (I did not put on any wt but this is just an illustraton). I am say the radio operator and got fat sitting around on the way North and the head man thinks and thinks and pretty soon he has no doubts about if he is going to eat me. All he is wondering is will I take much salt. Sunday nite they can have me for cold cuts. That is the way Harry is looking at me. Does he give a damn if I am the only one that can operate the radio and notify civilization? No. He is thinking I wd make a nice roast. The same with Harry. Is he thinking about the mice that come in because I work here? No. All he is thinking is how if I was not on the payroll it wd be the same as getting his electricity free.

Well I am a great student of human nature and always prided myself on reading characters, so I know Harry wd break my contract in a minute. If I was not

willing to break my contract then he wd get a
couple of hoods and I wd be in a taxi accident and
maybe break my knee cap. I will break a contract any
day in preference to my knee cap. So I sound out a
couple other spots but they say I want too much
money. I got desparate. I even went to one lug and
said I wd sing and run the floor show and also take
pictures. I did not have any kodak but anybody can
take pictures but even so they said no and I wd not
come down in price more than $25 a wk.

Well, what is an angle, I asked myself. Then because I always use to make my Easter duty and did
a lot of people favors I got my reward. They had this
busboy named Pablo that use to fix me up a sandwich once in a while and I befriended him by overhearing a tip on a horse at Arlington and it paid I
think around $18.40 and Pablo was on it for a fin. So
he always recalled that and one nite after Harry gave
me the explorer look I was having a sandwich and I
guess I was unable to disguise my feelings because
Pablo ask me what was the matter and I just said
nothing at all really. Just blue. And he tho't it was
some mouse but I said any time a mouse made me
feel that way he should let me know. I did not wish
to worry Pablo and did not inform him why I was
worried as I knew Pablo would worry too because
even if he did not know it his job was also in danger
and I wanted the poor chap to have his happiness.
Well he took away the dishes etc. and you know how
those people are and how nothing gets them down
for long. They bounce right back because they are
primitive and not very close to civilizaton like jigs.
So a minute after he was so sympatico Pablo was
humming away a tune. Well I was smoking and thinking and suddenly this tune gradually began creeping

into my thot's. It grew on me. Finally I asked him I
said what was the name of it and he smiled and said
it did not have any name. I said was it perhaps some
Mexican folks' song and he said oh, yes, it was six or
seven Mexican folks' songs all in one. He said it was
one of his own, which he made up out of a lot of songs
from his native land, Mexico. "Sing it again," I said.
He was very pleased and sang it all through for me.
Well I jumped up and as soon as the band finish the
set I went over to the piano and one fingered it and
wrote it out on the back of a menu card. But that
was not necessary because on the way home I remembered it and the next afternoon when I woke up I
remembered it.

Well you know how I am. Like Berlin. I can fake a
tune in one key so the next couple days I was down
at the joint in the afternoon playing it on the piano
till I had it all mastered and not any too soon I might
ad. Because the last afternoon I turned around and
saw the guitar player in the band standing there.
"How long of you been here, I said. He said he just
got there and I did not know whether to believe him
or not as he wd steal my tune as quick as look at me
but I did not want to let on it was important so I just
said play a few and he was like any ham mu-
sican and started in and played Muddy Waters. I
wanted to test him to see if he wd play my tune but
he didn't.

Well now I have something in case Harry the explorer decides to cut me up but the hell of it is I cant
trust any of these bastards and that is where you
come in. I know there is no larceny in you Ted boy so
what I am going to do is go to a music store and get
one of those recording machines and play the tune
and cut a wax of it. I will cut a couple and send one to

you so that if you lose it or anything I will still have
one and anyway that will show that it was my idea.
Then when I send it to you you play it over and see if
you think it has possibilites and if so maybe you can
get Johnny Mercer or somebody to write some lyrics
for it. I will guarantee to let you play it first over the
air and who knows but perhaps that is not a new
career for me, that of song writer. I have a lot of
ideas along this line and only need a little encourage-
ment. My tune can be played as either a rumba or
conga, fox trot or waltz. If I could get a good Ascap
rating this year I would quit this business in a minute
and stop worrying about Harry the explorer. So look
in the mail any day now for a record. Be sure and tell
your secretary that anything from me is to go to you
without opening it.

As always,
PAL JOEY

A Bit of a Shock

FRIEND NED:

Well Ted it may come like a bolt out of the blue sky me calling you Ned after all these years of you and I being mutual pals but why I called you Ned is because I wanted to prepare you for a surprise just like I got one about 2 wks ago. I had this little surprise around 2 weeks ago that I guess I certanly had it coming to me. In the ordinary course events a surprise comes from where you the least expect it and which is precisely what happened in my case. But dont worry as I do not intend to continue calling you Ned as you are Ted to me and the same old Ted and the same old pal Joey.

I menton above how where you least expect it etc. That goes double in spades and cards whatever that means. By double I mean in the 1st place *where*. The second place should be *how* and the third pl. *who*. Well where was a new crib where they had me rehearsing for a new show. I dreamed up a little comedy patter and a few stories like Joe E. Lewis and his little story about his cousin and the hot ferryboat but I guess I shouldnt of attempted that in Chicago as Chi. is where Joe E. got his start but that was just an error on my part and tho't they would of forgot the story by this late date. So anyway these gorills come

91

and ask me to work for them in this new room they
have, it being in the Loop dist. So being idle at the
time I gave my consent before either one of us had
time to change our mind. They tell me to come
around Thurs. and I do.

How is the story.

Who is the mouse in the story.

Therefore we have where, how and who.

So I am rehearsing and they have a line consisting
of six mice and only one of them you wd take to a
building excavaton, or else take all six of them there
and throw five of them in where it is deepest. It is the
kind of a line where they all do challenge dances to
make it look like they were all good hoofers or anyway make it seem like they had a line of 16 mice. The
mobbers who run the joint have a relapse and decided
to spend a small sum on advertising and that is how
this Melba comes into my life. Melba works on one
of these Chi. papers and there is very little doing in
the clubs in the summer and so when the papers get a
buck from club ads they like to play ball. So they decided to give us a little free publicity and send Melba
around to get an interview with nobody else but yr.
pal Joey. It is for the Sunday paper.

Well we are rehearsing and I am doing a patter
with the kids in the line where they come up to me
one by one and ask me what I want for Xmas and it is
all the double entender. But it is the way I play it
that is funny. I do not know exactly who to compare
myself with but for illustraton Maurice Chevalier. I
am having trouble with one of the mice because she
is mugging even in rehearsal and as far as I could
make out is doing her impresson of Kate Hepburn
and any minute will go into her impresson of L.
Barrymore. A poor man's Shiela Barret. In there

punching and trying to crab *my* act. So I gave up in disgust and went over and sat down till Duilio, the boss came over and asked me why and I said I was all in favor of giving a fugitive from Maj. Bowes a little helpful push but wd be God damned if I wd play straight for them when it is my own act. I said you people have gone out and spent money advertising that I was going to open as master of ceremonies and then some mouse getting $23 a wk comes along and you might as well not have me there as it is a waste of money. Get her to get her brother or old man free, I said and you won't have to pay me. Duilio agreed and said "Well I guess you are tired and why don't you take 15 minutes and during that time I will tell her and so I sat down and was having a quiet powder when in came something. I was tired and only raised my eyes when she came in but I tho't to myself Lesbo. I looked at her and tho't well so this is the kind of a joint I picked and did not know it. I tho't I could peg a joint like that from 2 mi. away and always did before but here I tho't I am all set to be m. c. in a crib where the Lesbos even come and watch the dress rehearsals. I am trying to give you the first impresson of this something. She is wearing this suit that you or I wd turn down because of being too masculine. Her hair is cut crew cut like the college blood. She is got on a pair of shoes without any heels and a pr. of glasses that make her look like she lost something but gave up the hope that she will ever find it. Then standing behind her is a little fat guy and when I first saw him I tho't now what the hell do these two do together. Then I got another look when she moved towards me and I saw he had a camera and I almost bursted out laughing. "They are going to make some postcards for their private collection, I tho't. Then the dame came closer to me and I was just about to cover my face with my hands and scream but then Duilio came over and said hello to her and shook hands and you wd think she was Mrs. Marshall Fields the way he bowed and cowtow to her. "What is this?" I said to myself, because Duilio is not double gaited as far as I knew but before I had a chance to do any more thinking he came over and introduced her to me and she gave me a slight brush and said okay let's sit over here and talk and she only had about a half an hour she said. Then Duilio menton that Miss so and so was the one that ran the night club dep't on some paper and gave me a punch in the ribs to con her into a good story.

Well we sat down and she ordered a double Scotch and water on the side and started out saying "What is a nice boy like you doing in a place like this?" Oh, a wise guy, I tho't. So I tho't I wd be a wise guy with her so I said it was okay if she wanted to look down on my job but I said some people have too much pride to go on relief and since I was able to entertain people with a few songs and stories I wd rather do that in preference to being just a bum. Oh, she said, you have pride and I said I was born with it. I said I had to quit college because the family lost our fortune and she wanted to know what college and I told her Dartmouth University. There I made a mistake. She said you never went to any Dartmouth and I said I ought to know and she said yes you ought to know they call it Dartmouth College and not Dartmouth u. I said when I was there we preferred to call it Dartmouth u. and she said yes, when you were there it probably was a university but you were never there yet. So she said let it pass and tell me about that family fortune that the family lost. Was it well up in 3 figures? I said

I was not brought up to boast about the am't of how much we had but if she wanted to know something when daddy blew his brains out in 1929 all the papers called him the millionaire sportsman and very sarcastically I said and of course the papers are always right. I said what did I know about how much he use to have? All I know was he left mother penniless. Sad, she said. Very sad. I said no not any more because mother was contented on the few pittances I was able to provide her and did not care any more about our fortune. I said may I ask where she went to college and she said she went to Mount Holy Oak. I said see the diff. bet. you and I. I said you bring up a place that I never heard of but I did not go ahead and deny there was any such place. I said the country is full of these small Catholic girls schools like Mount Holy Oak and I only had the greater respect for them being a Catholic myself on mother's side. Okay, she said.

I thought I made my impresson by putting her in her place but the more the fool I. I wasn't satisfied with the crap I handed her but had to put it on thicker and all this time she stopped asking me questons but just listened, me thinking she was taking it all in and that I had her spellbound with my stories about polo and yacting and our huge estate. Then all of a sudden she held up her hand like a traffic cop and said you can stop now before you run down. It is been fascinating and thank you but she did not have time for any more. I said what did she mean and she said "Pally I never heard so much crap in such a short time in my life. Such a fertle imaginaton it is a pity to be wasted in a nite club. I will wite my own story but it wont be as good as yrs. "Okay Moe, she said to the fat little camera man and he came over and then she called one of the mice and said something to her and the two of them went to the dressing room and about 5 min. later she came back but I did not know her. What she did was undergo a complete transformaton and took off her cloths and got into panties and brasserie that belong to one of the mice and took off her glasses and for the 1st time in many wks I forgot about Lana Turner. Yes that is how good this Melba was. Gams and a pair of maracas that will haunt me in my dreams and what is more when she got makeup on she was even pretty. I did not get the point but she said come on (to me) and put her arm in mine and posed like she was doing some kind of a dance step with me. She said Girl reporter at nite club rehearsal with new m. c. sensaton. Girl reporter lives life of nite club entertainers. She had me all over the place smiling and posing like we were dancing together. She said it was all pictures for the Sunday paper. Well I was a willing subject because anything to get my hands on her. All the time Moe kept taking pictures. Then she stopped and went back and got into her rags and by the time she was dressed and shoed and glassed again I recovered my composer. To think of this going around Chicago and never anybody knowing about it because of the disguise. I said I hope she wd come to the opening but she said she wd not be found dead in a nite club and got over that yrs ago so I said well I did not blame her because it was a shallow life &c. and said I wd like to talk to her some time about it and she burst out laughing and said dont waste yr time. You just got a little bit of a shock I am aware but you just saw as much as you will ever see so get rid of such ideas because among other things my husband use to play football at Dartmouth U. as you call it. He is also satisfactory in every other way and I must be running along. Its been nice knowing you &c. So how do you like that? It is like the primative savages that make their women wear viels right here in the 2d biggest city in the country. But I learned one thing to never judge a book by its cover and the only trouble is when I walk along the street I am always passing up the pretty mice and going on the make for the tired ones dressed like girl scout masters.

PAL JOEY

Reminiss?

FRIEND TED:

I was only thinking the other day how it is every once in a while I get home late at nite and as the old no. use to have it I climb the stair and nobody is there but me and my shadow and how because of our kind of an occupaton it is too late to call anybody but something for a fin or a deuce who will come up and entertain you. But not good enough. I guess what you do you stand there leading one of the Naton's No. 1 name Bands all nite and see Betty there all nite and wd. not apprisiate any but the best and the same with me. Here I am in Chi and some nice mice are in Chi and know a lot of the best and wd. not be contented with any but the best. That is what happens to the both of us. I give with the vocals and wolf around in a nite club and see the best and it is not good enough if I can call up the highest paid bag in Chi and get it for ½. Mostly at that time of the nite I want it for free and with love too at that.

Thence I look around my tiny nook of an apt. and see how I have a buck here & there hid in under the rug or a doz. Charvette ties from some souvenier of a romantic ideal. But feel sorry for my self all the same except when I happened to think I am also a man with a few good friends in this world and of them all there is none more highly prized than you Ted. Yes, I mean it. Some have the opinon that Joey, yr old pal Joey is a chap that if he did not have another breath of the body it wd be okay with them and they may be right. All of my life I did things that I wished I did not do because of hurting people like in Cincinatti that time we ganged that poor unfortunate mouse that you and I and also Kell went around with it in a sling for the best part of a yr. I recall that very distintly because of still getting bills from that quack in Pittsburg and if I were you Ted wd pay that little tab as he is getting nasty with me but you have a Name Band. Also the time when that lug in Pa. coal regons was trying to pay us off in the dark and was it you slugged him or me and we got in the bus and were in Maryland before he opened up his eyes. I wished I could reminiss about the time at the Penn State College which was some Prom and we took $50 off some College boy that wanted to have some summer job and we said we wd fix him with Waring. Well we had some great old times together you & I and I guess that is why when I get home some nites alone and wd. rather sit down and write to my friend Ted than waste my time on the phone winning some high paid bageroo.

That is exactly how the situaton is tonite and am sitting here and wish we had a jug of that corn stuff they gave us at the Virgina University and could talk it over and reminiss. I guess one time when we had a lot of fun was the time when we had the Battle of Music vs a college band the Barbury Coast Band from Dartmouth U. They said they were from Barbury Coast because of some reason I forget. But from Dartmouth U. I guess that was pretty nearly the 1st time I moved in on a society deb down at Webster

Hall in the village but it burn down. I seem to have recalled that we made the college boys play all nite or any way 2 hrs straight meanwhile you and I and Pete and Noodles and Chick moved in on the society debs. We were all kids then and tho't how it was tough to move in on a society deb and I guess we tho't we wd all end up with a Jordan roadster in those days. I said I was from Princeton, I remember that much. I did not even know if Princeton was in Phila.

Well friendship is a great thing especially in our occupaton where we never get home at a decent hr. I seem to have recall that one time we were booked in the old Ballaban & Katz Publix or I guess you were not along that time but it was just after you went with Goldkette and I went along with the band and Sparky Bosch took his wife along for some un-known reason that I will never be able to understand. Mike Shortridge was suppose to be ahead of the band then but doubling back and our best interest at heart till one nite we played the 1st show and went out and it was this town Chi. where I now am and we went out to pollute the lungs with fresh air and the shock of it or something he ate put Sparky right on the pavement, out like a light. They had to get somebody to take him home as we were on again in 5 mins. But by the time he got back to the flea bag where we were staying he felt okay but did not feel so okay when he went up to his room and discovered that Mike Shortridge and his little 2 wks old bride were in the kip and did not want to be interrupted by Sparky or any body else. I am sorry you missed that as Mike was around 50 yrs of age and Sparky around 21 but Sparky was always a fresh punk and Mike use to be a football star at Georga Teck. Sparky played a lot of horn in his day

but he never got a lip like he got from Mike. Mike is
a kind of guy that you dont interrupt him when he is
in the kip with a little 2 wks old bride even if it is yr
bride.

Do you ever think about the old days? I do. I read
the thing in the *Down Beat* about you about how at
30 you are still an old timer but maybe they meant
two timer or double timer or back timer (only kidding
Ted). I give them the same thing myself only they do
not ask me. I mean *Down Beat* does not ask me. But
in Chi. they do not recall I was here when Isham was
still here at the College Inn. I even wear a little rug
up front but so does the Grooner and Freddie
Astare. I can level with them and tell them I do not
know what they mean by the Loop because I wd
rather forget most of the times I was here before.
Jack Jenney and Carl Kress and Manny Klein go
right thru town and never give me a bell and I guess
they think they are hot stuff by so doing. But if you
want to know the truth I wish they wd never look me
up or give me a bell as the Chi people are of the
opinon I am a kid from the Princeton college and if
they see me around with Klein and Kress and Jenney
and like Freeman and them these Chi. people know
a lot about band guys and wd wonder how I knew
them so well. I cultivated young Bobby Hackett so
as I wd look younger when Hackett went thru here
with Horace Heidt. Christ I knew Bix. I read all this
stuff about Bix and how wonderful he was and all I
remember about Bix was the article I saw in the Life
mag. where Bud said he did not wash his feet. Well I
never saw Hackett with his shoes off but for my
dough he is a bare footed coal miner if that is the way
Bix got to play good cornet.

Friend Ted I was just thinking of a bad wk in Pa.

every summer for a couple summers. Do you remember Lakewood, Lakeside, Berwick, Schulkill Park, Reading, Mealey's in Allentown, Bach's in Reading, the Island nr. Harrisburg, Maher's in Shenadoh, Rocky Glen nr. Scranton, and Manila Grove near Tamaqua? Boy I could go on with them and so could you. I wish we had a chance to reminiss some nite even tho you are the leader of the Naton's No. 1 band. Not that I am not doing okay in Chi. because I am. I often think to myself that what if I turned out to be a Channcey Morehouse and a Dave Tough? That wd mean I was a really good drummer but not the lug that does not know a flammadiddle from a high hat. I put on such a good act here in Chi. that I kid myself and think I do not remember how to play Jazz Me. Jack Gallagher could sing it good and he only had one arm. I have both my arms so there is not any reason why I never sang it as equally as good. Do you recall the look of a surprise on Frank Trumbaur's kisser the nite I picked up an E flat and gave a slight job on Farewell Blues and he did not know I could play sax but also did not know that was the only thing I could play and the wart stood out as if he wanted to stab me with it. I ruined the reed that nite but always did not when I picked up an E flat alto but when I put it down. I guess this country is full of sax players that b't new reeds on acc't of me playing one chorus of Farewell Blues. Well you take a sax player and I will take a left handed pitcher. Put them all together they spell dixie.

Methinks I will not turn this missile over to the Post as it is just reminissing from here to Atlantic City but I had a lot of fun out of it writing a letter to my friend Ted without putting the arm on him for a couple of bucks. Ted the only all around honest decent guy I ever knew except for one or two instants that if some mouse was not mixed up in it wd not of happened. Ted you are a great guy and should of been a priest the way yr mother said. Ted old friend am waiting for a bageroo for free and could go on writing to you and reminissing from here to Atlantic City Steel Pier 10 wks guaranteed but methinks the bageroo is got her finger wedged in my doorbell. Will leave her wait a minute or two and teach her a good lesson not to get her fing. wedged in a gentleman's door bell at this hour of the night. If it is the one I called up she wd not miss a finger because she lost everything else when the boys came back with Gen. Dewey in the Span. American War.

Ted old friend how the hell are you and how does it feel to be rich?

Will bet you put yr dough into an insurance innuity and send the rest home to yr mother. I never saw you even pick up a tab for 4 mocha java coffees you cheap larceny jerk if there ever was one. I know you gave me the X X or otherwise I wd be making those so called wise cracks with Robin Burns every Thurs. and wd have my own stable of horses. It is a good thing I only write you letters instead of getting a hinge at yr holy kisser so I could hang a blooper on it. Friend Ted I am speaking to you and will tear this up but always was

Yr
Ex Pal Joey
(Hate yr guts)

The Libretto and Lyrics

PAL JOEY

HISTORICAL NOTE

This show was presented for the first time anywhere by George Abbott, December 11, 1940, at the Forrest Theater in Philadelphia. It opened December 25, 1940, at the Ethel Barrymore Theater, New York. That production had scenery and lighting by Jo Mielziner, dances by Robert Alton, costumes by John Koenig, and musical arrangements by Hans Spialek. It was staged by Mr. Abbott. I would like to mention the names of the persons in the company (on-stage). They were: Gene Kelly, Robert J. Mulligan, June Havoc, Diana Sinclair, Sondra Barrett, Leila Ernst, Amarilla Morris, Stanley Donen, Vivienne Segal (to be sure!), Jane Fraser, Van Johnson, John Clarke, Averell Harris, Nelson Rae, Jean Castro, Jack Durant, Vincent York, James Lane, Cliff Dunstan, Shirley Paige, Claire Anderson, Alice Craig, Louise de Forrest, Enez Early, Tilda Getze, Charlene Harkins, Frances Krell, Janet Lavis, Olive Nicolson, Mildred Patterson, Dorothy Poplar, Mildred Solly, Jeanne C. Trybom, Marie Vanneman, Adrian Anthony, John Benton, Milton Chisholm, Henning Irgens, Howard Ledig, Michael Moore, and Albert Ruiz.

The revival was presented by Jule Styne and Leonard Key, in association with Anthony B. Farrell, at the Shubert Theater, New Haven, December 25, 1951, and then at the Broadhurst Theater, New York, January 3, 1952.

The music, of course, is by Richard Rodgers.

J. O'H.

SCENES

The Action of the Play Takes Place in Chicago,
in the Late Thirties.

ACT ONE

ACT TWO

ACT ONE

Scene I

Cheap night club, South Side of Chicago. Not cheap in the whorehouse way, but strictly a neighborhood joint.

MIKE, the proprietor, is sitting at a table, stage left. JOEY has just finished singing:

JOEY

CHICAGO

There's a great big town
On a great big lake
Called Chicago.
When the sun goes down
It is wide awake.
Take your ma and your pa,
Go to Chicago.
Boston is England,
N'Orleans is France...

MIKE

Okay. Anything else?

JOEY

Sure.
   (*Does some dance steps.*)

MIKE

(*Stopping him*)

That's enough.

JOEY

Well?

MIKE

Well, I don't know. What do you drink?

JOEY

Drink? Me—drink? I had my last drink on my
twenty-first birthday. My father gave me a gold watch
if I'd stop drinking when I was twenty-one.

MIKE

Umm—so you don't drink. How about nose-candy?

JOEY

Nor that, either. Oh, I have my vices.

MIKE

I know that. Well, we have a band here. The drummer is just a boy.

JOEY

Hey, wait a minute.

MIKE

Okay. We got that straight. But we also have some
girls.

JOEY

Yeah. I know. I saw some of them.

MIKE

Oh, so that's it?

JOEY

I ran over the routine with them.

MIKE

I think they can handle you.

JOEY

Bet?

MIKE

Now, look. I don't know whether you're the man for the job or not. This job calls for a young punk about your age. About your build—about your looks. But he has to be master of ceremonies.

JOEY
(Starts to interrupt)

Listen . . .

MIKE

Don't interrupt. He has to introduce the acts, such as they are. He has to have a lot of self-confidence. He has to be able to get up and tell a story. He has to be sure of himself in case he gets heckled.

JOEY

Say . . .

MIKE

You—you're sure you wouldn't get embarrassed in front of all those strangers?

JOEY

Ah, I love you. I can talk to you. When do I start?

MIKE

Tomorrow night.

JOEY

What about my billing?

MIKE

What?

JOEY

Outside, the marquee. Billing. My name. My picture.

MIKE

Drop dead.

JOEY

Naw, Mike. It's good business for you. Why, last month when I was at the Waldorf-Astoria . . .

MIKE

Don't give me that.

JOEY

Huh?

MIKE

Now look, Laddie, I know all about you, so just try to get by on your merit and not on some tall story. The last place you was playing was a dump in Columbus, Ohio, and you got run out of town because you was off side with the banker's daughter.

JOEY

Oh, that.

MIKE

And the many other places you played have been very far from the Waldorf-Astoria, so just keep to the facts.

JOEY

All right, so I'm not a Crosby. But do these local clients know that? Look, you take my picture, blow it up, put it outside. My name up on the marquee. You never did that before?

MIKE

Not in this crib.

JOEY

That's the point. You never had anyone worth doing it for. But you start with me, and they think, "He must be some hotshot." They think good old Mike he's gone out and got himself a class act. And every night the rope's up.

MIKE

Just one bad night, and you'll be on the end of it. What about a front? You got a full dress? Tails?

JOEY

Tails? You know who wears tails? Dancers. Tony de Marco. Veloz, you know, Veloz and Yolanda. They wear tails.

MIKE

And I hear no complaints about *them.*

JOEY

Ah, but they're dancers. A dancer has to be that way, you know, formal, smooth, suave. (*Pantomimes dancers*) But not an M.C. The whole idea of an M.C. is to get people to relax, have fun, buy that wine, that bubbly. If an M.C. comes out wearing tails nobody has any fun. But I come out in my snappy double-breasted tuxedo, maybe I'm wearing . . .

MIKE

(*Cuts in*)

Okay. I'm beginning to think you gave the matter some thought. Okay. Maybe you're right. You wear your tuxedo.

JOEY

That's the talking. Now you're cooking with ee-lec-tricity. I think it's twenty-three bucks.

MIKE

What's twenty-three bucks?

JOEY

That's with the interest. I got twenty on the suit, but of course those guys aren't in business for love.

MIKE

Oh.

JOEY

Oh. Twenty-three, twenty-five.

MIKE

Remember, this means I'll keep you till the end of the week.

JOEY

Why, Mike, I consider myself a partner.

(Slaps MIKE on back. The KID enters and puts on shoes.)

MIKE

What about this rehersal?

KID

They're coming, Mr. Spears.

MIKE

Well—I'll be back later.

(Exits.)

JOEY
(Acting for the KID)

Ouch!

KID

What's the matter?

JOEY

Oh, it's nothing. I got a bad leg when I cracked up one time.

KID

Cracked up? You mean in an airplane accident?

JOEY

I used to have my own plane when I was nineteen or twenty.

KID

Oh, I'd love to be able to fly. I've never been up in an airplane, but I always wanted to.

(GLADYS *enters carrying her shoes, showing that her feet hurt. Unseen by* JOEY *or the* KID *she sits on the steps, rubbing her feet.*)

JOEY

It's my life. My love.

Oh, you get something out of flying that you don't get anywhere else. I sold my plane, but the chaps out at the airport let me fly for nothing. I'll take you up some time.

KID

Would you?

JOEY

Why, I'd be glad to. Next week, maybe. Tonight I might tell you some of my experiences.

GLADYS

(*Interrupting*)

Hey, Kid.

KID

Huh.

GLADYS

Get the rest of them in here.

KID

Okay.

(*She exits.*)

GLADYS

Now you're an aviator.

JOEY

What's it to you?

GLADYS

(*Mimicking him*)

Tonight I might tell you some of my experiences. (JOEY *sits*) The big aviator! Were you ever up in an elevator, for God's sake?

JOEY

You bore me.

GLADYS

What was that one you used to tell? How you were a rodeo champion?

JOEY

You bore me. Anyway, you never heard of me.

GLADYS

I heard about you. Remember that tab show you used to be in? My sister was in that show. I heard all about you.

JOEY

Yeah? Which one was your sister?

GLADYS

The one you didn't score with.

JOEY

That must have been the ugly one.

(SANDRA *enters.*)

GLADYS

You punk!

(*The* KID *enters with five other girls.*)

KID

Okay, Gladys.

GLADYS
(*To* JOEY)

You sing the first vocal—I come on for the encore.

JOEY

Right. Where's the rest of them, and the waiters?

MICKEY
(*Entering*)

Hey—on the floor—everybody.

DIANE
(*Entering*)

Say—didn't you used to be in Pittsburgh?

JOEY

I was everywhere.

DIANE

I was sure I saw you at the Band Box, singing.

GLADYS

Skip the old-home week.

JOEY

(*To* DIANE)

Later, honey. (*To all. Girls begin to take off work
clothes*) Now, children, the same routine we did earlier.
If you're all good, put everything in it, maybe I'll form
a Joey Evans unit, and take you all over the country.
Now get your places, and let's have some co-operation.

(*Music cue.*)

JOEY
YOU MUSTN'T KICK IT AROUND

I have the worst apprehension
That you don't crave my attention.
But I can't force you to change your taste.
If you don't care to be nice, dear,
Then give me air, but not ice, dear.
Don't let a good fellow go to waste.
For this little sin that you commit at leisure
You'll repent in haste.

REFRAIN

If my heart gets in your hair
You mustn't kick it around.
If you're bored with this affair
You mustn't kick it around.
Even though I'm mild and meek
When we have a brawl,
If I turn the other cheek
You mustn't kick it at all.
When I try to ring the bell
You never care for the sound—
The next one may not do as well.
You mustn't kick it around!
    (MIKE *enters.*)

MIKE

Hey, Joey, come here.

JOEY

Yeah, Mike. (*To Girls*) Go ahead, keep on rehearsing.

(MIKE *and* JOEY *exit.*)

GLADYS

Keep on rehearsing, that's what he thinks.

SANDRA

My feet hurt.

WAGNER

What does he think this is, the Follies?

KYLE

This is a hell of a way to make a living.

FRANCINE

Rehearse all day and work all night.

ADELE

You're lucky you got a job.

FRANCINE

Oh yeah.

ADELE

Yeah.

DOTTIE

Hey, look at her—Miss Ambitious 1935.

DOLORES

My mother told me.

AD LIB

My mother told me.

SANDRA

I used to get by just showing my shape. Now I have to dance my fanny off for fifty bucks a week.

GLADYS

You said it.

WAGNER

Wish I was tall enough to be a show girl, then I wouldn't have to dance.

GLADYS

You ain't kidding.

DOTTIE

Who did you ever think I saw yesterday?

SANDRA

Who ever?

DOTTIE

Muriel, ever. She's working at Marshall Field's.

SANDRA

What as?

DOTTIE

Floorwalker.

SANDRA

Don't talk dirty.

MIKE
(*Enters. To Girls*)

Come on—get up—you heard Joey. Keep on rehearsing.

GLADYS
(*An aside*)

This crumb is but *really* taking over.

MICKEY

Me, I think he's cute.

GLADYS

Who *don't* you think is cute?

MIKE

Come on—come on—keep rehearsing.

GLADYS

REFRAIN

If my heart gets in your hair
You mustn't kick it around.
If you're bored with this affair
You mustn't kick it around.
Even though I'm mild and meek
When we have a brawl,
If I turn the other cheek
You mustn't kick it at all.
When I try to ring the bell
You never care for the sound—
The next guy may not do as well.
You mustn't kick it around!
(*Dance. Blackout. Traveler closes.*)

ACT ONE

SCENE II

A girl is standing in front of the pet shop. This is played by LINDA ENGLISH. *She is looking through window of pet shop, toward audience.* GIRL *comes from left and exits, right.* MAN *enters, left—looks at dogs, tries to make them—exits, right.* GIRL *followed by* MAN *enters, right, and exits, left, quickly.* JOEY *enters from left. He is wearing his dinner jacket, over it a trench coat with collar turned up. He is sauntering along, takes a second look at the girl, and stops and looks in the window.* LINDA *does not look at him, but moves over to make room for him. He is giving her sidelong glances, but she pays no attention. Then:*

JOEY
(*In that dog-babytalk*)
Hel-yo Skippy. Skippy boy. (LINDA *looks up, but now he pays no attention*) Hel-lo, boy. You wish you were outa there, doncha, boy?

LINDA
(*Involuntarily*)
Oh, I'll bet he does.

JOEY
Sure, he does. Aah, these people, they don't care about dogs. What do they know about dogs? A puppy

—why, to them a puppy is fifteen dollars, twenty dollars, whatever will make a profit for them.

LINDA

Oh, some of them are nice to the dogs.

JOEY

Are they? If they are I never met them. They put on an act for you, but they have no interest in any dog. Looka that little fellow, the wire-haired, the one I call Skippy.

LINDA

He's cute, he's sweet.

JOEY

Well bred, too. Hy, Skippy.

LINDA

Oh, you mean that one? I thought you meant the wire-haired one.

JOEY
(*Trapped*)

Well, he's a wire-haired Scotty. Don't you know anything about dogs?

LINDA

No. I just love them.

JOEY
(*Relieved*)

I don't know. You can't really love dogs if you don't know a little about them. A wire-haired and a Scotty, they're just about the same family—terriers.

LINDA
(*She looks at him*)

I never really thought of that, but I guess it's true.

JOEY

(*Stronger*)

Hyuh, Skippy.

LINDA

Why do you call him Skippy? Is that his real name, or did you have a dog called Skippy?

JOEY

That's it.

LINDA

Which?

JOEY

I had one called Skippy. (*She leans forward and he inspects her figure some more*) I'd rather not talk about him.

LINDA

Oh, tell me something about him. I never had a dog myself. Wouldn't you like to talk about him?

JOEY

Well, you understand, this was an Airedale I used to have. Oh, he wasn't much. We had champion dogs in those days. That was when the family still had money.

LINDA

Your family?

JOEY

Sure. Mother breeded dogs for a hobby.

LINDA

Huh?

JOEY

Well, sort of a hobby, the way Daddy played polo!

LINDA

Oh.

JOEY

Well, one day I came home from the Academy. I was going to an academy then, about ten miles from the estate. I didn't learn much there, except how to play polo and of course riding to hounds. So this particular day I have reference to, I was returning to our estate. They opened the gate for us and about a mile up the road I saw Skippy coming. Oh, he could always tell the sound of the Rolls every afternoon. Of course, the poor old codger was half blind by that time, but we gave him a good home. So I was sitting up with the chauffeur and I saw Skippy coming. He was up near the main house, about a mile or so, and I instructed the chauffeur, I said—Chadwick—be careful of old Skippy, and he said—yes. But with Skippy you couldn't tell, because his eyesight was so bad. Well—do you want to hear the rest of it?

LINDA

Did you run over him?

JOEY

It wasn't the chauffeur's fault, really. Not actually. But Daddy discharged him anyway. Mother erected a monument over his grave. (*She cries*) Skippy's, I mean.

LINDA

Oh.

JOEY

I guess it's still there unless they took it away. I never go back. (*She looks at him*) The estate fell into other hands when Daddy lost his fortune. That was when I resigned from the Princeton College. Hy-yuh, Skippy, boy.

(*Looks at her.*)

LINDA

Oh.

JOEY

Don't cry . . . (*Arm around her*) That was a long time ago.

LINDA

I know, but I mean, first your dog, and then losing your fortune.

JOEY

Yes, I never go by the house on Park Avenue without I have to laugh. Ha. (*He laughs*) I soon found out who my friends were.

LINDA

You mean fair-weather friends? Just because you lost your fortune?

JOEY

Not only that. I guess you don't recognize me. Well, that's a lucky break too.

LINDA

Why?

JOEY

Daddy. He was never brought up to work. He never did a day's work in his life, so when the crash came he took the only way out, for him. I don't think he was a coward. That way Mother got some insurance.

LINDA

Oh, how awful. And what about you?

JOEY

Down, down, down. I M.C. in a night club over on Cottage Grove Avenue. That's where I've ended up. Do you live around here?

LINDA

Yes. With my sister and her husband.

JOEY

Oh ... Apartment?

LINDA

Yes, I sleep on the living-room couch. That is, till I get a job.

JOEY

Living-room couch. You have a car?

LINDA

No.

JOEY

No car.

LINDA

Sometimes my brother-in-law lets me drive his.

JOEY

I didn't mean to bore you with the story of my life.

(*Music cue.*)

LINDA

Oh, I wasn't bored. I feel honored that you confided in me. I hope you tell me some more.

JOEY

I probably will. You inspire me. You know what I mean?

I COULD WRITE A BOOK

A B C D E F G,
I never learned to spell,
At least not well.
1 2 3 4 5 6 7,
I never learned to count
A great amount.
But my busy mind is burning
To use what learning I've got.
I won't waste any time,
I'll strike while the iron is hot.

REFRAIN

If they asked me I could write a book
About the way you walk and whisper and look.
I could write a preface on how we met
So the world would never forget.
And the simple secret of the plot.
Is just to tell them that I love you a lot;
Then the world discovers as my book ends
How to make two lovers of friends.

Second Chorus—

LINDA

Used to hate to go to school,
I never cracked a book
I played the hook.
Never answered any mail,
To write I used to think
Was wasting ink.
It was never my endeavor

To be too clever and smart.
Now I suddenly feel
A longing to write in my heart.

(*Repeat CHORUS*)

ACT ONE

SCENE III

The Night Club. LINDA *and a* BOY FRIEND *are at table,
left. Girls do Chicago Number.*

GIRLS

CHICAGO

There's a great big town
On a great big lake
Called Chicago.
When the sun goes down
It is wide awake.
Take your ma and your pa,
Go to Chicago.
Boston is England,
N'Orleans is France,
New York is anyone's
For ten cents a dance.
But this great big town
Oh that great big lake
Is America's first,
And Americans make
Chicago.
Hi ya boys.

(Repeat)

(*When the number is over,* MIKE *rushes to the waiter, right.*)

MIKE

Table, get a table ready. (*To* JOEY) Lay it on good, now, Boy.

JOEY

What?

MIKE

Mrs. Simpson's outside. She's coming in.

JOEY

Who?

MIKE

Mrs. Chicago Society. Mrs. Prentiss Simpson.

(VERA *enters with escort and couple, they go right, sit.*)

JOEY
(*Continuing*)

Well, ladies and gentlemen, that's our show. That is, our *midnight* show. We have another complete show going on again at two o'clock. At two o'clock we have Beatrice Lillie, Clifton Webb, Noel Coward, Gertie Lawrence and a whole mob coming down from some other big party (*To* LINDA) *Hi ya.*

LINDA

See, Harry, isn't he cute?

JOEY

Oh, I forgot. This party wasn't here in time to catch the whole thing. (*Crossing to table, left.*) Well, I'll tell you about our show. First, I come out, and tell a few stories. Of course, if you want to sit home and listen to Bob Hope, you'll hear the same *stories*. Of course, you don't get the music of Jerry Burns and his Pneumatic Hammer Four over the *radio*. Ah-ha no, and if your luck holds out you never *will*. No, but seriously, folks, Jerry has a swell band, and I think they're going places. Go places, will you, boys, you *bother* me. (*His foot business.* VALERIE *enters, right, and crosses, right center*) Oh, my God!

VALERIE

Can I recite now?

JOEY
(*To Vera's table*)
I have to explain this to you latecomers. Valerie does a dance, doesn't she, *folks?* (*Howl*) You see what Valerie has on now? Well, that's what she starts with in her dance. What a beautiful dancer! We had a guy here one night—well, I'll tell you one thing about him —he came here, and he came alone. So he watched Valerie dance—right down to the last rose-petal, and you know what he said when she finished?

ALL (*Ad lib*)

No.

JOEY
You wanna know?

ALL (*Ad lib*)

Sure—yes.

JOEY
He said—"She doesn't know how to keep time." She doesn't know how to keep time! Well, we found out later he was waiting for the *drummer*. (*Noise from Band*) Only fooling, Bob. Well, after that is our big

production number. Do you want to wait for it? Valerie will wait, won't you, dear?

VALERIE
Now can I recite?

JOEY
No! (*Laughter and applause*) Seriously, ladies and gentlemen, the next show'll be on in just a little while, and it's entirely different. Thank you. Now there will be a short intermission. (*Music from orchestra.* JOEY *comes to* LINDA's *table.*) Hello, pretty little Miss English. How are you? You like the vocal?

LINDA
Oh, yes. I thought it was pretty wonderful. Really.

JOEY
You know why?

LINDA
No—why?

JOEY
Because I was singing it for you.

LINDA
Oh—Why, you didn't even see me. You didn't even know I was here till after you finished singing.

(MIKE *crosses to* JOEY.)

JOEY
Ah—I didn't say that. All I meant was I was thinking of you. You can't deny that.

(MIKE *gives* JOEY *message from* VERA.)

LINDA
I have a job, too.

JOEY

Excuse me, I gotta talk to some people. A pleasure . . .

(*To* LINDA's *boy friend. He crosses to* VERA's *table, right.*)

VERA

Hello. Won't you join us? Mr. Armour—Mr. Swift. (JOEY *sits*) Why haven't I seen you before?

JOEY

That's easy. You never been here before.

VERA

That's perfectly true, but I get around. I've been to just about every other night club in Chicago, and of course, New York. Didn't I read outside that you were direct from the Jamboree Club on 52nd Street?

JOEY

Could be, could be.

VERA

Well. I was there last month.

JOEY

Lady—a secret—I was never there. Not even as a customer.

VERA

Why, that's fraudulent. It's dishonest. Joey Evans direct from Jamboree Club. Name up all over the place. Pictures. Are you a Chicagoan?

JOEY

No.

VERA

Oh, you're going to be difficult. Secretive.

JOEY

Sure. If I give it to you all at once you wouldn't come back.

VERA

You're about the freshest person I think I've ever met. What makes you think I care enough to come back?

JOEY

Lady, you can level with me. You'll be back.

VERA

(*To one of the gents*)

Shall we go? I don't like this place.

JOEY

Wait a minute. I'm liable to get the bounceroo if you walk out like this.

VERA

You worry about that.

MIKE

(*Angry*)

So?

JOEY

So what?

MIKE

Absolutely from hunger less than five weeks ago, and the first time we get some live ones in the joint you can't keep your hands to yourself.

JOEY

My hands? Why don't you stop?

MIKE

Then if it wasn't your hands, you said something. Wuttid you say?

JOEY

She did the talking.

MIKE

Any spot in town would give a week's take to have her come in. So she picks my lousy crib by some accident, and what do you do? You give her the business like she was some kid on the line. You're not only out. You're out all over town. Here—(*Starts peeling off bills*) and get out of here before I start wrecking my own furniture.

JOEY

(*Follows him*)

Wait a minute. So, maybe I did talk a little out of turn. She started it.

MIKE

Stop it.

JOEY

I'll make you a bet. If she doesn't come back in, say, two nights, you can give me the bounce without paying me a nickel.

MIKE

Which is a good idea for now. Here—take your moola.

JOEY

Two nights. Tomorrow night, or the next night. What can you lose? Either you win my pay, or, if she does come back—you know how they are. They'll keep coming back, and spending—wine money.

MIKE

Well, maybe. I'd like to know your angle.

JOEY

No angle. A job and ... (*Shrugs.*)

MIKE

You're kidding. That dame? Mrs. Prentiss Simpson?
Come on. Wuttid she say?

JOEY

Ah, no. When I have more to tell you, maybe I'll tell
you. (*To himself*) And believe me, if I have nothing
to tell I'm gonna make it good.

(*Exits.*)

(*Fanfare.*)

MIKE

Ladies and gentlemen—we now present our next
number—Okay, bring on the girls—

(*Girls enter for Rainbow Number from down left.*)

GLADYS

THAT TERRIFIC RAINBOW

My life had no color
Before I met you.
What could have been duller
The time I went through?
You lowered my resistance
And colored my existence.
I'm happy and unhappy too.

CHORUS

I'm a red-hot mama
But I'm blue for you.
I get purple with anger
At the things you do,
And I'm green with envy
When you meet a dame,

But you burn my heart up
With an orange flame.
I'm a red-hot mama
But you're white and cold.
Don't you know your mama
Has a heart of gold?
Though we're in those gray clouds
Some day you'll spy
That terrific rainbow
Over you and I.

(Dance routine.)

GIRLS

Though we're in those gray clouds
Some day you'll spy
That terrific rainbow
Over you and I
That terrific rainbow
Over you and—

GLADYS

Skiddlee vuten—daten daten

GIRLS

Yeah, yeah.

(VICTOR enters.)

(Dance—VICTOR and GLADYS. All exit, left.)

GIRLS
(Entering from left)

(ENCORE)

Though we're in those gray clouds
Some day you'll spy
That terrific rainbow

Over you and
Dad dee do, dad dee do.

GLADYS
I'm a red-hot mama

GIRLS
Oh skiddle dee boo—Yeah!

(*Girls exit, right.* GLADYS *and* VICTOR *exit, left.*)

BLACKOUT

ACT ONE

Scene IV

JOEY *at the phone, right.* VERA *at the phone, left.*

JOEY
(*Into phone*)

Hello, Miss English there? Oh, how are you? This is
your pal Joey. You know, your contact with café society. I just called up to ask what happened last night,
why'd you leave so suddenly. . . . No, no. You got it all
wrong. I hadda go an' talk to those people. They own
the place. Not exactly own it but maybe they're gonna
put a little money in it. All right, so I didn't look as if I
ever saw them before. I didn't. But that's the way it
is . . . *What* middle-aged woman . . . Hello, hello. . . .
(LINDA *has hung up*) Oh all right, small fry.

> (*He starts to dial as the lights dim. When they
> are out, the phone rings on the opposite side of
> the stage. The lights pick up* VERA *as she takes
> the phone.*)

VERA
Yes, Mr. Evans, from New York—Oh, of course.
Hello, Norton?

JOEY
Hello, Vera. How are you?

142

VERA

When did you get in?

JOEY

Just a minute ago. How's Prentiss?

VERA

What did you say.

JOEY

I said, how's Prentiss?

VERA

(*Frowning*)

Is this Norton Evans?

JOEY

Uh-huh.

VERA

Well, I don't believe it is. You'll have to identify yourself. Uh-h-h. What was the name of the play we saw in New York last summer?

JOEY

Why, I think we saw 'The Man Who Came to Dinner."

VERA

Oh, you do. Well, Norton Evans and I haven't seen each other for over a year, and Norton Evans calls my husband Pete. Now, who is this please?

JOEY

All right. (*Laughs*) This is Joey Evans.

VERA

Who?

JOEY

You know. Last night.

VERA

Oh. The night-club thing.

JOEY

That's right. Listen, I just thought I'd tell you what I think of you. You know you cost me my job. I'm through the end of this week, not only here, but all over town. They tell me you're such hot stuff around this town you can keep *anybody* from working. Well, it's a lousy town anyway, but I just thought I'd tell you to go to hell before I leave.

VERA

WHAT IS A MAN

VERSE:

> There are so many, so many fish in the sea,
> Must I want the one who's not for me?
> It's just my foolish way
> What can I do about it?
> I'm much too used to love—
> To be without it.
>
> What is a man:
> Is he an animal,
> Is he a wolf,
> Is he a mouse,
> Is he the cheap or the dear kind,
> Is he champagne or the beer kind?
>
> What is a man:
> Is he a stimulant,
> Good for the heart,
> Bad for the nerves,

Nature's mistake since the world began.
What makes me give,
What makes me live,
What is this thing called man?

Hello, Jack—can't keep the appointment,
Have an awful cold (*sneeze*)
Hello, Frank—
Have to meet my husband.
So long—please don't scold
Hello—Hello—Love.

What is a man:
Is he an ornament,
Useless by day,
Handy by night,
Nature's mistake
Since the world began?

They're all alike,
They're all I like,
What is this thing called Man?

ACT ONE

Scene V

The night club again after the last show. On stage:
JOEY, WAITER, SWEEPER.

WAITER
(*To* SWEEPER)
See the boxes go downstairs.

(*Exits.*)

(JOEY *puts out cigarette on floor.* SWEEPER *calls him S.O.B. under breath—sweeps cigarette off.* JOEY *takes chair off table and sits. Kids are on way home. One of them sneaks up behind him and puts her arms around him.*)

SANDRA
I hear you're getting the bounceroo.

JOEY
You hear good, Gladys.

SANDRA
Huh?

JOEY
Oh, I thought you were Gladys.

SANDRA
Oh. You thought I was Gladys. I was gonna ask you

to come up to the apartment, but if it's with you and Gladys well nutsa to you-a. You had it coming to you.

(*She goes off.*)

DOTTIE
(*Furtively*)

Don't whatever you do call me tonight. My husband's back.

JOEY

Just my luck. Let me know when he goes back on that baker wagon.

DOTTIE

What do you mean baker wagon? He owns a piece of a band. You're pretty fresh for somebody that's washed up. *I* heard.

(*Exits.*)

(GLADYS *on her way out.*)

JOEY

Hey, Gladys—no good night?

GLADYS

Listen to what's talking. If I let you come home with me tonight there'd be no getting rid of you. *I* heard.

JOEY

You mean about me going to the El Morocco in New York?

GLADYS

What?—El Morocco. You'd have to join the Foreign Legion to get to Morocco.

JOEY
(*To* VALERIE)

How about you, you bum?

VALERIE
(*Crossing, right, to exit*)
Who are you calling a bum? You bum.

MIKE
(*Crossing down to* JOEY)
Well, wise guy. One more night. You and Mrs.
Prentiss Simpson. (*Knock—Knock.* MIKE *goes up steps*)
Nobody here. Everybody went home. (*Starts down.
Knock—Knock*) Aw, nuts.

> (*He goes up steps and out of sight to open
> door.*)

VERA
(*Off stage*)
Good evening.

MIKE
(*Backing in*)
Come in, Mrs. Simpson.

> (*Goes to foot of stairs.*)

VERA
My, what a nice reception.

> (*Coming down. Followed by gent.*)

MIKE
Sorry we're all closed up, Mrs. Simpson. (*Gent
staggers.* MIKE *catches him*) But I can fix you up with
a powder. (*Gent starts for table, left*) A little drink.

> (*Gent staggers and* MIKE *takes him to table—
> hold for next line.*)

VERA
I'd love one. I like it like this. It's so peaceful (*Gent
sits*) Why, Mr. Evans.

JOEY

Hello.

MIKE

(*Gesturing to* JOEY, *who has remained seated*)
Up. Up.

VERA

No, don't bother. Mr. Evans is tired, I'm sure. He has to work on his Valentines. Did you know about Mr. Evans and his Valentines, Mr. uh—I never knew it, so I did not not get it.

MIKE

Spears. Just Mike is all right. I get no respect around here, so I guess you can call me Mike too.

VERA

All right, Mike were you serious about that powder?

MIKE

I sure was. Has to be Scotch. Everything else is locked up.

VERA

Scotch and plain water is fine for me. (*Looks at her companion*) Nothing for him.

MIKE

(*To* JOEY, *as he goes off*)
I don't pay off yet.

VERA

So I can go to hell?

JOEY

You can double go to hell. You know what else you can do?

VERA

Something about a galloping rooster, I imagine?

JOEY

Why the hell couldn't you come back earlier?

VERA

Why earlier?

JOEY

Never mind. Skip it.

VERA

Why earlier? Oh I'll bet I can guess.

JOEY

Guess your head off.

VERA

You told Mike that I'd be back. Didn't you?

JOEY

Why, the heel.

VERA

No. I've had no conversation with Mike. Give me credit for some intuition. After all I am a woman.

JOEY
(*Giving her the "eye"*)

Yes, I'll say that for you.

VERA
(*Drawing herself "together"*)

Intuition and mind changing. I decided last night . . . that I'd never come here again. Tonight I change my mind. Oh, I can tell you the whole story. When we walked out of here last night Mike was annoyed because he counted on our spending a lot of money . . . Right so far?

JOEY

Go ahead.

VERA

So he fired you, but you said, "She'll be back, I know her kind." Right?

JOEY

I said, go ahead.

VERA

You thought it over. "How can I get her to come back?" By the way, how'd you get my number?

JOEY

Easy. The press agent of this joint has a 1919 Social Register.

VERA
(*Slapping his face*)

1919 eh? . . . Well, to continue, you thought of the technique of the insult. Instead of appealing to my better nature, which you are sure I do not possess— Does it hurt? I hope?—you reveal yourself as a sensitive, understanding young man. And it worked. That's why I'm here. (JOEY *rises—then sits again*) But one moment, please. One moment. The reason it worked isn't because I was sucker enough to get angry. Oh, no. The reason it worked, dear Mr. Evans, was that you were nice enough to treat me differently. Or is that a subtlety that escapes you? No matter. (*She rises*) However, one thing you must never never never forget. I'm older than you, and I'm a very smart and ruthless woman, so don't try any fast ones. Come on.

JOEY

Where to?

VERA

Oh, you know where to. You knew it last night. Get your hat and coat. I'll be waiting in the car.

(MIKE *enters carrying bottle as* VERA *starts to exit.* JOEY *gives* MIKE *the "fingers" and exits.* MIKE *gestures you S.O.B. with bottle.*)

MIKE
(*To Gent, left, bottle on table*)
Hey, you—you wanna get plastered? Oh.

DOTTIE
(*Entering*)

The hell he is.

GENT
(*Coming to*)

Where is she?

DOTTIE
What's the matter with Joey?

MIKE
You know as much about it as I do.

DOTTIE
He says he's going hunting.

MIKE
Hunting?

DOTTIE
That's what he says.

MICKEY
(*Entering*)
He says he's through with this dump.

GENT

(*Rising*)

Where is she?

MIKE

(*Taking Gent off, left*)

Come on, brother.

DOTTIE

What does he mean? Why should Joey be through?

GIRL

(*On from right*)

I don't know. Why don't you ask him.

(JOEY *enters, center.*)

DOTTIE

Joey, are you leaving?

(JOEY *enters—shakes "no."*)

JOEY

HAPPY HUNTING HORN

Don't worry, girls,
I'm only on vacation
Not out of circulation,
Don't worry, girls.
Don't worry, girls,
While I still have my eyesight
You're going to be in my sight;
Don't worry, girls.
You never can erase
The hunter from the chase.

REFRAIN

Sound the happy hunting horn.
There's new game on the trail now:
We're hunting for quail now,
Happy little hunting horn.
Play the horn but don't play corn,
The music must be nice now,
We're hunting for mice now,
Happy little hunting horn.
Danger's easy to endure
If you're out to catch a beaut:
Lie in ambush, but be sure
When you see the whites of their eyes—don't
   shoot!
Play the horn from night to morn,
Just play, no matter what time,
Play, "There'll be a hot time!"
Happy little hunt—bang! bang!—ing HORN.

(Dance. JOEY *exits.)*

*(Second Chorus—Boys enter—Dance—Travel-
er closes.)*

ACT ONE

SCENE VI

Tailor Shop. Counter with samples on it. On stage:
JOEY, ERNEST.

ERNEST

I like this, lots.

JOEY

Yeah, who's wearing this?

ERNEST

Well, of course no one is. Everything is exclusive. If you bought this you'd be the only one, but Mr. Teddy Winston, the polo player—well, he has a jacket quite a little like it.

JOEY

Okay. Make up a suit out of it.

ERNEST

The trousers too? I thought just the jacket and possibly some contrasting slacks.

JOEY

The suit. The schmeer. What else do I need?

VERA
(Enters)

Hello.

155

JOEY

You're late enough.

VERA

You better get used to it, my pet. This stuff—thank goodness you didn't buy any of this.

JOEY

What? I bought all of it.

VERA

Oh, no you didn't. Now, Ernest, didn't he tell you I sent him here? You wouldn't do this to a friend of mine, would you?

ERNEST

Had I but known, Mrs. Simpson. But the gentleman never mentioned your name.

VERA

Well, that's something. All right, throw all the stuff away and we'll start from scratch. And can I scratch!

ERNEST

Very good, Mrs. Simpson. Very good. Now I have some new ... If you'll just step this way ...

VERA

And don't show us any more of Teddy Winston's stuff. (*To* JOEY) If you started dressing like a gentleman you might begin behaving like one, and that I but never could take. Stay as sweet as you are, dear.

JOEY

That's the way to do it.

VERA

Do what?

JOEY

Keep me as sweet as I am—pamper me a little.

VERA

Somebody started that a long time ago.

JOEY

Well, it got results.

(*He exits, left.*)

(*Music cue.*)

VERA

BEWITCHED, BOTHERED AND BEWILDERED

VERSE:

He's a fool, and don't I know it—
But a fool can have his charms;
I'm in love and don't I show it,
Like a babe in arms.
Men are not a new sensation,
I've done pretty well, I think;
But this half-pint imitation
Puts me on the blink.

REFRAIN:

I'm wild again!
Beguiled again!
A simpering, whimpering child again!
Bewitched, bothered and bewildered am I.
Couldn't sleep
And wouldn't sleep
Until I could sleep where I shouldn't sleep.
Bewitched, bothered, and bewildered am I!
Lost my heart, but what of it?

My mistake, I agree.
He's a laugh but I love it
Because the laugh's on me.
A pill he is,
But still he is
All mine and I'll keep him until he is
Bewitched, bothered, and bewildered
Like me!

SECOND CHORUS:

Seen a lot;
I mean a lot—
But now I'm like sweet seventeen a lot.
Bewitched, bothered and bewildered am I.
I'll sing to him—
Each spring to him,
And worship the trousers that cling to him.
Bewitched, bothered and bewildered am I.
When he talks
He is seeking
Words to get off his chest.
Horizontally speaking
He's at his very best.
Vexed again
Perplexed again
Thank God I can be oversexed again
Bewitched, bothered and bewildered am I.

(VERA *crosses, left and sits.*)

THIRD CHORUS:

Sweet again
Petite again
And on my proverbial seat again.
Bewitched, bothered and bewildered am I.

What am I?
Half shot am I.
To think that he loves me
So hot am I.
Bewitched, bothered and bewildered am I.
Though at first we said no sir
Now we're two little dears
You might say we are closer
Than Roebuck is to Sears.
I'm dumb again
And numb again
A rich, ready, ripe little plum again
Bewitched, bothered and bewildered am I.

(JOEY *and* ERNEST *enter. Look at sample.*)

LAST ENCORE:

You know—
It is really quite funny
Just how quickly he learns
How to spend all the money
That Mr. Simpson earns.
He's kept enough
He's slept enough
And yet where it counts
He's adept enough.
Bewitched, bothered and bewildered
Am I.

JOEY

Why didn't you come with us? Don't you take an interest?

VERA

I'll see the final result.

(LINDA *enters. She is a stenographer and has*
something for ERNEST *to sign*)

LINDA

Will you okay this, please, Mr. Ernest?

JOEY

Hyuh. How're the dogs?

LINDA

Oh, I never get a chance to see them any more. I
moved. I'm not in that neighborhood any more.

JOEY

Oh.

(VERA *starts tapping her foot, which* ERNEST
notices. He shoos LINDA *away.*)

ERNEST

Go away, Miss Birnbaum, or whatever your name is.
(*To* VERA) She's new here. (*To* LINDA) I told you never
to . . . (*To* VERA) Or perhaps you'll excuse me just a
second? It might be important.

LINDA

It isn't important, Mr. Ernest. (*To* JOEY) *Good-bye.*

(*She goes off.*)

JOEY

Good-bye.

VERA

Now really.

JOEY

I only saw her twice before in my life. She likes
dogs. (*Laughs*) Imagine that. She's crazy about dogs.
Ordinary dogs, that you see in a window.

VERA

And that's how you got together. You—Albert Payson Terhune, you. Oh, I can just see you, with your pipe, and your Teddy Winston tweeds, and a stout walking stick, tramping across the moors. (JOEY *laughs*) What are you laughing about?

JOEY

Those moors. I used to work in a band with a guy named Moore. I'd like to tramp across him.

VERA

Stop it. Anyway, this, uh, mouse, as you call them. (*Shakes her head slowly, warningly*) No. See? No . . . Good God, I'm getting to talk like you.

JOEY

Her? That's jail bait. Of course she'd old enough to work . . . How old do you have to be to work in this State?

> (VERA *looks off stage, sort of wondering whether to do anything about the mouse,* LINDA.)

VERA

At what?

JOEY

Ah, you're not listening. How about this one? (*He picks up some material as another mouse comes on. He does not see the mouse, but* VERA *does and misinterprets what he says*) I like this one.

VERA

Oh, you do, eh?

JOEY

Yeah . . . and it ought to wear like hell. About a hundred and twenty clams.

VERA

(*As mouse exits*)

And how did you know it was a hundred and twenty clams?

JOEY

It says so. Look. (*Holds up tag*) See?

VERA

I didn't. But I do now. Oh, what you missed.

JOEY

What did I miss?

VERA

Never mind. You probably only missed it once. Anyway it's the evening things that are important. You never get up in the daytime. If you're going to be a great big master of ceremonies, in a great big night club...

JOEY

Hey, I thought it was going to be aan-teem. Small but exclusive. Chez Joey. Chez Joey. I can just see myself in white tie, and tails, maybe an opera hat sort of like this . . . (*Imitates a smooth toothy entrance*) "Maysure a dam." Suave. I bow here, I bow there. Very quiet. Maybe I have the plumbers playing Valentina very soft behind me. Never raise my voice. I wish I could do it all in French. Maybe I will, maybe I will.

VERA

Maybe you better not.

JOEY

Maybe I better not. Tonight it is my pleasure—to—present—for your delight . . . Hey, maybe a sort of a patter. Tonight—it is my pleasure—to present for your delight—Bazum, bazum bazum zum, bazum bazum, bazum. Hey, how about that? Who writes that kind of stuff? Maybe I could get him to grind out a little thing like that.

VERA

Bazum.

JOEY

No, sugar. No cracks.

VERA

Bazum. Get your mind off bazum.

JOEY

You wrong me. You wrong me. I'm only thinking of my work. Anyhow you put all this scratch in an-teem little cloop. Is that right? Cloop?

VERA

Club, Joint, Dive, Crib, I don't care what you call it.

JOEY

I like cloop. Anyway, you put all this moola in the cloop, I want it to be a success for your sake, honey sugar. I like to think of your investment.

VERA

Just remember, my hero, that it is my investment.

JOEY

What have I done that you don't trust me?

VERA

What have you had a chance to do?

ERNEST
(*Enters*)
So terribly sorry, but I . . .

VERA

Never mind, Ernest. The important thing is the evening clothes. Not too Brooks Brothers. After all, he's only a boy and we want to keep him looking that way. But on the other hand, not too, you know, lapels and things.

JOEY

I guess I can order my own clothes.

VERA

That's what I mean. Whenever he tries putting in his ideas, that's when to be very careful.

ERNEST

I think I understand, perfectly. Now if we'll just go in the fitting room.

(ERNEST *and* JOEY *go.*)

VERA

Don't mind me. I'm leaving. (LINDA *enters with some notes in her hand. She passes* VERA *as though to go after the men*) Oh, you're new here, aren't you?

LINDA

Yes. My second week.

VERA

(*Putting on the "tough act"*)

Well, would you mind telling Ernie to be sure and put the extra-size pockets in for the guns? My husband is kind of absent-minded and he forgot the last time.

LINDA

What?

VERA

Imagine that lug, forty suits he ordered and not a Goddamn one with a rod pocket in it.

LINDA

Your husband?

VERA

Did you see him or didn't you? He's in there with
Ernie now. I gotta scram. Take a note. Quote. Joey
Evans stuff. Be sure and put in extra revolver pockets.
Unquote.

LINDA
(*Tearfully making notes*)

Yes, ma'am?

VERA

Okey doke. Oh yeah. Tell him I gotta talk tough
to his first wife. She wants more alimony. More alimony! (*Walking, right.*) She's lucky to be alive, that
babe. Well, be seeing you.

(*Exits.*)

LINDA

Be seeing you—thank you.

ERNEST
(*As he and* JOEY *re-enter*)

. . . But I could have guessed to the quarter inch . . .
Thirty-eight and a quarter shoulders, left shoulder
slightly higher . . .

JOEY
(*Paying no attention—to* LINDA)

Hy yuh, babe. I guess you don't sleep on that living-
room couch any more since you got a job.

LINDA

No, sir. (*To* ERNEST) You're not to forget about the
revolver pockets in this gentleman's suits.

JOEY AND ERNEST

Revolver pockets?

LINDA

And your wife said to tell you she's going to talk tough to your first wife. About the alimony.

JOEY

What *is* this?

LINDA

I'll bet you never ran over Skippy. I'll bet you shot him.

(*Exits.*)

ERNEST

But Mr. Evans ...

JOEY

Ah—let it alone. (ERNEST *exits*) She can't bother me; nobody can.

(*Music cue*)

PAL JOEY

What do I care for a dame?
What do I care for a dame?
Every old dame is the same.
Every damn dame is the same.

I got a future—
A rosy future;
You can be sure I'll be tops.
I'm independent;
I'm no defendant.
I'll own a night club that's tops
And I'll be in with the cops.

What do I care for the skirts?
What do I care for the skirts?
I'll make them pay 'til it hurts.
Let them put up 'til it hurts.

I'm going to own a night club;
It's going to be the right club.
For the swell gentry—
It's elementary
I'll wear top hat and cane.
In Chez Joey,
They'll pay Joey,
The gay Joey—
I can see it plain.

(*Traveler opens*)

(*Ballet.*)

ACT TWO

Scene I

VICTOR is standing, center, looking at the costumes of two girls. MICKEY is at left center.

STAGE MANAGER

Hey, Scholtz!

SCHOLTZ
(In wings)

Yeah.

STAGE MANAGER

Hit Gladys with a surprise pink.

SCHOLTZ

Okay.

VICTOR

And when I say pink light, I mean pink.

VALERIE

I'll tell him.

STAGE MANAGER

Hey, Scholtz!

SCHOLTZ

Yeah.

169

STAGE MANAGER

You'll have to raise that baby when they bring those tables on the floor.

SCHOLTZ

Right.

VICTOR

Oh, don't worry about that. We're never gonna be ready to open tonight.

VALERIE

I'll tell him.

VICTOR

You keep your mouth shut.

DOTTIE
(*At entrance, with three Girls*)
Is this all right, Victor?

VICTOR

Come here. Where's Mr. Evans?

(*Examines costumes.*)

MIKE
(*Entering*)
Don't bother, Joey. I got him slated for an interview in fifteen minutes. Get your opening number cleaned up first.

STAGE MANAGER

Give me the trim.

SCHOLTZ

Okay.

VICTOR

Where's Gladys?

MICKEY

Getting on her costume. She'll be here in a minute.

VICTOR

Well, hurry her up.

VALERIE

I'll tell her.

(*Exits.*)

DELIVERY BOY
(*Entering with crate of eggs*)

Want this in here?

MIKE

No, never mind. Take it downstairs.

STAGE MANAGER

Stand by and lower that border.

GLADYS
(*Entering, giving "Mi-Mi-Mi" with the voice.*
VICTOR *crosses to left of her to see her costume*)

Did you reserve that table for those friends of mine?

MIKE

All taken care of.

GLADYS

Can they see the floor? I mean with a telescope.
Have 'em good, will you? They're very important people.

MIKE

I bet.

VALERIE
(*Re-entering*)

Victor!

VICTOR

What is it?

VALERIE

They're ready.

VICTOR

It's about time. All right, on your toes, everybody. I want no interruptions—and no noise. (*Hammering off stage*) And try to get it right just once. All right, Louis, on the bench.

(*Flower Number*)

THE FLOWER GARDEN OF MY HEART

LOUIS
(*The Tenor*)

I haven't got a great big yacht,
But I'm contented with my lot,
I've got one thing much more beautiful and grand.
I do not own a racing horse.
But that don't fill me with remorse.
I possess the finest show-place in the land.
So come with me and wander.
To a lovely spot out yonder.

REFRAIN

In the flower garden of my heart
I've got violets blue as your eyes,
I've got dainty narcissus
As sweet as my missus
And lilies as pure as the skies.
In the flower garden of my heart
I've got roses as red as your mouth.
Just to keep our love holy
I've got gladioli

And sun flowers fresh from the South,
But you are the artist
And love is the art
In the flower garden of my heart.

RECITATIONS—FLOWER NUMBER

Violet—the flower dear old grandmother wore
Away 'way *back* in the days of yore.

Sunflower—the favorite of white and dusky pixie
Away down south in the land of Dixie.

(*Sunflower:* "*I'm a sunflower*")

Heather—Sir Harry Lauder sang of its beauties—
The decoration of all Scotch cuties.

Lily—the flower of youthful purity—
It's very sweet—you have my surety.

Lilac—the sky turns blue and the churchbells
chime.
Ah—love—we love sweet lilac time.

If you're a hundred percent American—goodness
knows
You love the American Beauty Rose.

REFRAIN

GLADYS

In the flower garden of my heart
I've got daisies to tell me you're true.
Oh, the west wind will whisk us
The scent of hibiscus
And heather that's smothered with dew.

In the flower garden of my heart
I've got lilacs and dainty sweet peas.

You will look like Sweet William
And smell like a trilliam
Surrounded by fond bumble bees,
But you are the pastry and I am the tart
In the flower garden of my heart.

(*After Flower Number*):

VICTOR

All right, strike those props and get everybody ready for the next number.

(*Ad lib on exit. Singer crosses from right to left taking off costume. Also Girls. Men set tables and chairs.* MIKE *enters with* MELBA.)

MIKE

Hey, Victor.

VICTOR

What is it?

MIKE
(*To* VICTOR)
Tell Joey to come out here.

VICTOR

Yes—yes.

MIKE
(*To* MELBA)
Sit right down here, Miss Melba. (MISS MELBA *sits*. JOEY *enters*. MICHAEL *crosses to* JOEY) Joey! Here's one I can leave you alone with.

JOEY

Alone? Here? That?

MICHAEL

Be nice. This is the press. You know. Publicity. Chez Joey's name in the papers.

JOEY

Ah?

MICHAEL

Her name is Melba Snyder. She's on the *Herald* . . .
Miss Snyder, make you acquainted with Joey, of Chez
Joey.

JOEY

Miss Snyder. Miss Melba Snyder, of course?

MELBA

Yes, as a matter of fact, but how did you know?
I usually only sign M. S.

JOEY

And I think it's a shame they don't let you sign your
whole name. (*To* MELBA) Just a second, Miss Snyder.
(*Aside to* MICHAEL) Oh, Michael, before I forget it,
in that second number . . . (*Voice lowering*) What
the hell does this dame do? Write a cooking column
or something?

MICHAEL

You're doing fine, boy. She does night-club news
and interviews.

JOEY

(*Faking for* MELBA's *benefit*)
Right. Then I come on for the last eight bars, right?

MICHAEL

Right.

JOEY

Sorry, Miss Snyder, but you know all this confusion
and helter-skelter and etcetera on opening night. Now,
as I was saying when Michael interrupted me, they
oughta let you sign your whole name. I often think, you

newspaper people—I don't know many of the ladies
and gentlemen of the press here in Chicago, but of
course New York. I know all the boys. Anyway, you
ought to have a *union*.

MELBA

We have a union.

JOEY
(*Covering*)
And I'm glad. Let's have a powder. (*Whistle. Calls*
WAITER) Waldo! You drink, of course.

MELBA

A double Scotch and plain water. No ice. Make that
St. James Scotch and tell him not to give me Jameson's
Irish.

JOEY
(*Dumbfounded*)

What?

MELBA
(*To the* WAITER)
Double St. James and water, no ice. And don't bring
me Jameson's Irish. (*To* JOEY) I can't drink Irish except straight.

JOEY
(*Weakly*)

Coke with lime.

(WAITER *exits.*)

MELBA

This is going to be a Sunday piece, so we can go all
out. You can start at the beginning, wherever you want
to. I never take notes, so go right ahead.

JOEY

Well, how I got in this business and so on?

MELBA

That's right.

JOEY

That was rather innaresting, how I got in this business. I was up at Dartmouth University—

MELBA

What for?

JOEY

Going there. I was a "soph."

MELBA

I thought they called it Dartmouth College.

JOEY

Sometimes we do, and sometimes we don't. It's a hell of a big place.

(WAITER *with drinks.*)

MELBA

Relatively. About 1650 students, I thought. Nothing to compare in size at least with Chicago, Northwestern, our universities. However, you were up there.

(*She takes a drink.*)

JOEY

As a soph. I was living at the Frat House.

MELBA

Frat?

JOEY

Sure!

MELBA

You make it sound like one of those colleges where Betty Grable's always going. But—continue.

JOEY

Well. The kids were sitting around singing and playing the piano and there was this society singer from New York—I grew up with her—Her name was Consuelo Van Rensselaer, Connie. I grew up with her, but I didn't see her much after Daddy lost his fortune. (MELBA *chokes on her drink*) We had to give up the estate. All the horses, and mares, and dogs . . .

MELBA

And?

JOEY

And yes, Miss Snyder—and bitches—we had to give them up too.

MELBA

Oh, yeah?

JOEY

Well, we had to give them all up when Daddy lost his fortune.

MELBA

You said that. Or maybe you forget. I'm not taking notes—I remember everything.

JOEY

We were sitting around singing all the old songs. Dardanella, Who. The oldies. Suddenly everybody stopped singing and I was the only one. It was a lovely old tune that Mother used to sing to me before going out to some big society ball. Mother had a lovely voice.

MELBA

That was before you lost your fortune?

JOEY

Yes. Exactly. She lost her voice when Daddy lost our fortune. The shock—(*Looks at her— thinks as though he is being ribbed—and continues a little mad*) Well, this lovely old tune . . .

MELBA

You don't happen to remember what it was called? Was it—(*Singing*) *Frère Jacques—Frère Jacques?*

JOEY
(*Cutting in*)
I believe it was. Yes, I believe it was.

MELBA

Oh, then everybody joined in.

JOEY

No—nobody else knew it.

MELBA

Oh.

JOEY

So Connie was sitting in a corner, and she was crying softly to herself. It reminded her of something. It was just the mood it got her into. So when all the others applauded, she sat there crying softly.

MELBA

Then did she say—you ought to be singing professionally, and introduce you to Pops Whiteman, and he gave you your first break, then you sort of sang with several other bands, and in night clubs, and that's how you happened to come to Chicago? Okay. I'll write it.

JOEY

Say, what is this?

MELBA

Let me make it up. You'll only confuse me. I have to get some pictures of this tripe. God knows why—God knows and I think I do—(*Looks at watch*) Cherist-mas—I've gotta leave. Good luck, and give my love to Connie Van Rensselaer.

MICHAEL
(*Enters*)

How's our boy doing? Giving you all the facts?

MELBA

He's given me plenty of information. I don't know about the facts.

JOEY

I'd like to interview you some day. You'd get plenty of information.

MELBA

I'd love it.

(JOEY *exits*.)

MICHAEL

Ah—you mustn't mind him . . .

MELBA
(*Crossing*)

Him? After the people I've interviewed? It's pretty late in the day for me to start getting bothered by the funny ones I talk to.

MICHAEL

Like for instance?

(*Music cue*.)

ZIP

I've interviewed Pablo Picasso
And a countess named di Frasso.
I've interviewed the great Stravinsky,
But my greatest achievement is the interview I had
With the star who worked for Minsky.
I met her at the Yankee Clipper
And she didn't unzip one zipper.
I said, "Miss Lee, you are such an artist,
Tell me why you never miss.
What do you think of while you work?"
And she said, "While I work
My thoughts go something like this:

REFRAIN

Zip! Walter Lippmann wasn't brilliant today.
Zip! Will Saroyan ever write a great play?
Zip! I was reading Schopenhauer last night.
Zip! And I think that Schopenhauer was right.
I don't want to see Zorina.
I don't want to meet Cobina.
Zip! I'm an intellectual.
I don't like a deep contralto
Or a man whose voice is alto.
Zip! I'm a heterosexual.
Zip! It took intellect to master my art.
Zip! Who the hell is Margie Hart?

SECOND CHORUS

Zip! I consider Dali's painting passé.
Zip! Can they make the Metropolitan pay?
Zip! English people don't say clerk
They say clark.

Zip! Anybody who says clark is a jark.
I have read the great Cabala
And I simply worship Allah.
Zip! I am just a mystic.
I don't care for Whistler's Mother,
Charley's Aunt, or Shubert's brother.
Zip! I'm misogynistic.
Zip! My intelligence is guiding my hand.
Zip! Who the hell is Sally Rand?

THIRD CHORUS

Zip! Toscanini leads the greatest of bands;
Zip! Jergen's Lotion does the trick for his hands.
Zip! Rip Van Winkle on the screen would be
    smart;
Zip! Tyrone Power will be cast in the part.
I adore the great Confucius,
And the lines of luscious Lucius.
Zip! I am so eclectic;
I don't care for either Mickey—
Mouse and Rooney make me sicky.
Zip! I'm a little hectic.
Zip! My artistic taste is classic and dear—
Zip! Who the hell's Lili St. Cyr?

(VICTOR enters.)

VICTOR

Michael.

MICHAEL

Well, what now?

VICTOR

There's a fellow out there to see you.

MICHAEL

Don't let him in.

VICTOR

I think he's going to come in whether we want him
to or not.

LOWELL

(*Off stage*)

Out of my way. (*Enters,* MICHAEL *enters, left, crosses
to right, and calls* JOEY *off stage.* JOEY *enters from
right as* LOWELL *enters from upper left.*) Mike, take
five.

MICHAEL

Hello . . . Hey you, waiter, Waldo . . . Nail them
tables down. Nail everything down.

LOWELL

Aah ha ha ha . . . Ah, you Mike. You're my guy.
(JOEY *enters*) You really are my guy. Let's sit down
over here after you introduce me to the new idol of the
airwaves. My name is Ludlow Lowell.

MICHAEL

Ooh. You really go by that?

LOWELL

It's my name. Cook County says it's my name.

MICHAEL

I know, but just amongst us kids. What is that again?

LOWELL

Ludlow Lowell, with two l's. Next year I change it
to Lowell with one l. It's a combination I figured out
on numerology and the stars, astrology. Sagittarius.

JOEY

Say it again, with two l's.

LOWELL

Lowell.

JOEY

Now say it with one l.

LOWELL

Lowell.

JOEY

I like it better with one l.

LOWELL

Oh, a fresh punk. Okay, Mike, it's your joint, I guess. But would you mind, you know, going away? Take a powder the hell outa here. Now. (*Crossing to table*) I take off my watch, I put it on the table here, and I ask you to shut up and listen to me for a minute. Okay? Okay. Now, I am a man of few words and very taciturn. I have a point and head straight for it, provided certain parties do not interrupt. Don't even say all right—just keep quiet.

JOEY

All right.

LOWELL
(*Rising*)

You spoiled it. Now I have to start all over again. (*Sits*) Okay. Watch on table. Man of few words. *So*— The word reaches me that an unknown is suddenly opening up in this newly decorated and refurbished decor. I ponder it over and consider it in my mind. Why? Well, Joey, if I know one thing it is night clubs

and human nature and who backs shows and the like
of that, and so I never heard of you, and so I add it all
up and deduce that you have a friend. Is this friend
a man? Maybe. Or is it a mouse?

JOEY
(*Interrupting*)

But I don't see how . . .

LOWELL
(*Rising, annoyed*)

How do you like the guy? He won't let you talk.
(*Sits again*) Well. All this I check up on through my
underground sources. I am not a gossip or a scandal-
monger that does not mind their own business, Joey,
but just incidentally I happen to hear who it is. Holy
hell—I say to myself. So I come right over to see if
you have representation.

JOEY

Are you asking do I have an agent?

LOWELL

"Representation" is what I offer.

JOEY
(*Rising—crosses away to left*)

I don't need any agents.

LOWELL
(*Taking contracts from pocket*)

Sign this.

JOEY
(*Crossing up*)

I sign nothing.

LOWELL

If I can assure and guarantee you $50,000 a year inside of a year and a half, is that any encouraging inducement?

JOEY

I'll be making that myself in that time without any agent.

LOWELL

Sign this, you God-damn pig-headed fool or I'll walk out on you.

JOEY
(*Over table*)

Why should I sign what I never even read?

LOWELL

Ludlow Lowell is why. Me. Take a quick gander at it. It is not typewritten. It is printed. It is a standard contract. (*Snatches it away from* JOEY) Here, give it back to me. I don't care if you sign it or you don't sign it. (GLADYS *enters*) Don't round now, but isn't that Gladys Bumps over there?

JOEY

Without looking, yes.

LOWELL

Gladys, darling. Come here and sit on my lap, Gladys.

GLADYS
(*Rusing to him*)

Louis—I mean Ludlow. (*Sits on his lap*) What's with you?

JOEY
(*Seated*)

You know this jerk?

GLADYS

You're the only one that doesn't know him. Are you wasting your time with the laddy-boy, here *Ludlow?*

LOWELL

That I fear, Gladys, that I fear. I have offered him representation; I have offered him a contract and he wants to *read* it.

GLADYS
(*To* JOEY)

Well, sign it, you jerk, before he walks out on you. Or have you changed your mind in the last ten minutes and no longer care for money?

JOEY

You think I ought to sign with this guy?

GLADYS

In blood, if necessary.

(JOEY *signs both copies.* GLADYS *and* LOWELL *exchange looks.*)

LOWELL

Gladys, would you care to attest this instrument? (*She takes*) Don't look at me that way, Gladys. I only mean do you wish to sign this as a witness?

GLADYS
(*Laughing*)

Oh, I thought ...

LOWELL

Don't worry, Gladys, we know what you thought. Lower left-hand corner. Two copies. (*She signs and he gives* JOEY *one copy*) Now then, old chappie, Monday afternoon three o'clock you come to my temporary office at the Morrison Hotel while I'm having the main office redecorated and refurbished. (GLADYS *exits*) You be there at three o'clock and we will have a little chat to get acquainted, and following that I am taking you over to NBC to audition for the Staff o' Life Bread program. (JOEY *rises as though to go*) By the way, a delicate matter, but you will tell Mike to send me your checks hereafter since I am representing you; then I put them in our special Joey account and deduct my small fee.

JOEY

But I got this job myself.

LOWELL

(*Has risen—pats his face*)

Contract's a contract, Joey. Let's not start right off on the wrong foot, you know?

JOEY

You're sure about this Staffo thing?

LOWELL

It is only the beginning. Thirteen weeks is the most I will sign for, that's how I feel about it.

JOEY

(*Crossing to him*)

Okay. How'd you . . . What made you think I'd be such a sure thing for this program? Who owns Staffo?

LOWELL

Are you kidding? Only Prentiss Simpson owns it.

JOEY

(*Slowly crossing, right*)

Oh...

LOWELL

I guess you know him? Or anyway, you know who
he *is*.

JOEY

Well, I gotta blow.

(*Exits.*)

LOWELL

Sure. Be seeing you, pally. (MICHAEL *enters*) Michael—a million thanks for the use of the hall.

MICHAEL

In the meantime, you wouldn't be upset if we went
ahead with our rehearsal?

(*Girls and Boys enter.*)

LOWELL

On the contrary, I want you to rehearse, because I'm
going to be here tonight, and I know it's gonna be
good.

MICHAEL

Okay. Now can we use the floor?

LOWELL

Don't worry, it'll be a smash!

SANDRA

How do you know?

LOWELL

It figures—numerology and the stars—Sagittarius—
Now I go.

(LOWELL *exits.*)

MICHAEL

Okay, kids. Go ahead and rehearse.
(*Dancing introduction followed by number
sung by* GLADYS *and* ENSEMBLE.)

PLANT YOU NOW, DIG YOU LATER

GLADYS:

Sweetheart, the day is waning,
Must go without complaining,
Time for Auf Wiedersehning now.
Right now it's time to start your
Farewells that mean departure
I keep deep in your heart
You're all for me.
Call for me soon.

REFRAIN

Where's the check?
Get me the waiter.
I'm not going to stay.
Plant you now, dig you later,
I'm on my way.
My regret couldn't be greater
At having to scram.
Plant you now, dig you later,
I'm on the lam.
Bye-bye, my hep-chick,
Solid and true.

I'll keep in step, chick,
Till I come digging for you.
So, little potater
Stay right where you are,
Plant you now, dig you later
Means au revoir,
Just au revoir!

ACT TWO

SCENE II

JOEY's apartment. He is on love seat, left, reading his notices. VERA enters from left at rise.

VERA

Well, Beauty, how did they treat you?

JOEY

They all said I was there. That's something, I guess. (VERA *eases to behind* JOEY) They didn't even say I stink. They didn't say anything except this newcomer from New York drew a fashionable crowd, and so forth. You got more out of it than me. Mrs. Prentiss Simpson gave a large party! And then the names of those jerks. Mrs. Prentiss Simpson was ravishing in a dirty old suit of tired overalls. Then the names of some more jerks. Yeah? When do I get my notices? I need my notices when I talk about my radio job.

VERA

I wouldn't worry about the job, Beauty.

JOEY
(Turns to her)

I'm thinking that over. That Beauty. I'm not sure I like it. I'm not exactly beautiful.

192

VERA

Listen. I'm over twenty-one. I know what's beautiful.

JOEY

Oh—I see what you mean. You—me ...

VERA

Don't analyze it. If you take it apart you might not be able to put it together again.

JOEY

Beauty, hey—nobody ever put it that way before.

VERA

I can believe that. Your average conquest—I imagine they were rather unthinking. Or else they never thought of anything else. And judging by the way some of my friends were looking at you last night ...

JOEY
(*Eagerly*)

Yeah? Which ones?

VERA

Oh, no. (*Rises*) Maybe not any place else—but here it's just you and I. While we're here I can be reasonably sure of you. That's why I'm really beginning to like this terrible apartment.

JOEY

Terrible apartment? Why, this is the *nuts*.

VERA

Yes, dear.

IN OUR LITTLE DEN

VERA: Just two little love birds all alone
        In a little cozy nest

With a little secret telephone,
That's the place to rest.

JOEY: Artificial roses 'round the door—
They are never out of bloom—

VERA: And a flowered carpet on the floor
In the living room.

REFRAIN

BOTH: In our little den of iniquity
Our arrangement is good.

VERA: It's much more healthy living here,
This rushing back home is bad, my dear,

JOEY: I haven't caught a cold all year:

VERA: Knock on wood!

BOTH: It was ever thus, since antiquity,
Down to you and me.

VERA: The chambermaid is very kind,
She always thinks we're so refined,

JOEY: Of course, she's deaf and dumb and blind—

BOTH: No fools, we—
In our little den of iniquity.

SECOND REFRAIN

BOTH: In our little den of iniquity
For a girly and boy,

VERA: We'll sit and let the hours pass,
A canopy bed has so much class,

JOEY: And so's a ceiling made of glass—
Oh, what a joy!

BOTH: Love has been that way, since antiquity,
All the poets agree

VERA: The radio, I used to hate,
But now when it is dark and late
Ravel's Bolero works just great.
That's for me.

BOTH: In our little den of iniquity.
       (*Dance*)
BOTH: Oh what joy
       (*Dance*)
JOEY: We're very proper folks you know.
VERA: We've separate bedrooms comme il faut.
       There's one for play and one for show.
BOTH: You chase me
       In our little den of iniquity.

ACT TWO

Scene III

Chez Joey, two days after opening. GLADYS *is lolling in a chair.* DOORMAN *is admitting* LINDA *at street door.* LINDA *is in street clothes and carries a package.*

Ad Lib:

VICTOR
I'll never be able to understand you, Gladys.

GLADYS
Be gone—be gone—I'm tired.

DOORMAN
(*To* GLADYS)
Here's somebody wants to see Mr. Mike.

GLADYS
What am I supposed to do?

LINDA
I have a C.O.D. for Mr. Evans but I'm supposed to collect the money from Mr. Mike.

DOORMAN
I'll tell him.

(*Exits.*)

GLADYS

Why don't you sit down? Mike is never in a hurry to pay for a C.O.D. Especially for Joey—I mean Mr. Evans.

LINDA

(*Sitting down*)

But after all, Joey is the star attraction.

GLADYS

He's the star. I'm not so sure about the attraction.

LINDA

What'd he ever do to you, or shouldn't I ask?

GLADYS

Well, nothing. He never really did anything to me, I guess.

LINDA

I don't believe anybody's all bad.

GLADYS

Aw, now listen. I'm tired.

LINDA

Oh, I'm not just a dumb Pollyanna, either. But Joey —if the right person took an interest in him maybe the good things would come out.

GLADYS

Then for my dough the right person took an interest a long time ago, and all the good things came out, permanently.

(VALERIE *enters from outside.*)

VALERIE

Hey, Gladys, there's a gentleman wants to see you. He says to tell you Ludlow is here.

GLADYS

Oh, lend me your coat. (*To* LINDA) Excuse it, please!

(*Takes* VALERIE'S *coat, and exits.* DOORMAN *enters.*)

DOORMAN

Mike says to wait for him in the office. In there.

(*Indicates office.* LINDA *goes there.* DOORMAN *gives her the eye, leering.*)

VALERIE

Oh, you been working in these joints so long, you think anybody with clothes on is pretty.

(LOWELL *enters, followed by* GLADYS)

LOWELL
(*To* VALERIE)

Could we talk a little private?

VALERIE

Who? Us?

LOWELL

Not this time, dear. I and Gladys this time.

VALERIE

All right.

(*Exits.*)

LOWELL
(*To* DOORMAN)

Hey you, you know what you can do.

DOORMAN

Yes, sir?

LOWELL

Walk east. Walk east as far as you can. You come to Lake Michigan. Keep right on walking till your hat starts floating. You catch?

DOORMAN
(*As he leaves*)

I catch.

(*Exits.*)

LOWELL

God, the help in this town are getting fresh and impertinent.

GLADYS

What's the scheme? Give.

LOWELL

Well, there's an ugly, ugly word for it. It is called blackmail or extortion in some sets. In our set it is known as the shake.

GLADYS

Do I get under the bed? Don't forget what happened the last time.

LOWELL
(*Smiling placatingly*)

Not this time. This time you're high and dry. I am only keeping you in reserve. Now if you let me expostulate the strategy, it's this way. This Mrs. Simpson. Joey's protector? Well, did you ever take notice to these trucks around town with Staffo on the side in big letters?

GLADYS

What would I be doing looking at *trucks?*

LOWELL

Maybe some day you'll be sorry you didn't, if one comes along with your number on it. Anyway, Staffo means a kind of bread. It is made by *Mister* Simpson in large quantities. I tell you how large the quantities are. One of these trucks that you never took notice to, they cost anywhere from three to ten thousand dollars each. Mr. Simpson has around a hundred of these trucks. Does that make an interesting mathematic to you? Is that a kind of an arithmetic that fascinates you?

GLADYS

(*Thinking*)

Say they're worth three grand apiece ... Why, that's $300,000 bucks. And he has to have people drive them, too. That costs money.

LOWELL

Right.

GLADYS

He has to have a garage to keep them in.

LOWELL

Right.

GLADYS

Gas. You can't run those trucks without gas.

LOWELL

Right. Right. Maybe I better help you a little if we're ever gonna get to the point. The important part, they carry a lot of bread, and he probably nets a cent on each and every single loaf of bread.

GLADYS

And then there's pie and cake, too.

LOWELL

Yes, dear. There's pie and cake and cinnamon buns and ginger snaps. Okay, he sells a lot of that stuff. Now get the psychology. A man that runs a bank . . .

GLADYS

Oh, a bank too? That's good.

LOWELL

Kindly refrain from opening your God-damn trap till I finish. Now look. A man that runs a bank, he has to be respectable till he gets caught. Then they get another man. But the man that sells bread or milk, the public thinks of him as a handsome old fluff with a white suit and a white cap on his head. If he gets in a jam, that's bad. They don't only get a new man. They get a new bread. The jam kills the bread. Ooh, what am I saying? Excuse it. So anyway, this is a two-way blackmail. I go to old Simpson. I tell him his wife is carrying on with my sister's fiancé.

GLADYS

Who's your sister?

LOWELL

You are my sister. Joey is your fiancé. If he don't get up the dough we are going to sue his wife, so that puts him in a jam. The other part, I'm a little ashamed of it, it's so old-fashioned. All I do, I go to Mrs. Simpson and just say if she don't get up say twenty Gees, I'll tell her husband about Joey.

GLADYS

I like that one better.

LOWELL

(*He starts to laugh*)

Oh, I almost forgot. This is such small change, but it strikes my sense of humor.

GLADYS

What's that? See an old lady hit by a trolley car?

LOWELL

No. In addition to taking Mr. and Mrs. Simpson, I decided just for the hell of it to take Joey too. (*They both laugh*) First we take dear Mrs. Simpson, then Joey ...

(LINDA *appears.*)

GLADYS

(*As* LINDA *crosses their table*)

You get everything straightened out?

LINDA

Yes, everything's straightened out.

GLADYS

I didn't hear any screams.

LINDA

That's nothing, I didn't hear you scream either.

GLADYS

Get her. Get that dialogue ... Oh, you ever meet Ludlow Lowell, the agent?

LOWELL

Artist's representative.

LINDA

How do you do and good-bye.

(*Exits.*)

LOWELL

Good-bye, good-bye.

(*Crosses to center, looking after* LINDA.)

GLADYS

You don't think?

LOWELL

No. Nobody ever hears me. I talk in a whisper.

GLADYS

You know this shake may not be so easy.

LOWELL

Don't worry. Let me make the plans. And I think our plan is to contact the charming Mrs. Simpson right away.

GLADYS

But I do worry. Remember that time I was found under the bed?

LOWELL

Forget it. It's very seldom you're found *under* the bed.

SANDRA
(*Enters*)

Come on, break it up. Joey wants us to rehearse that corny Morocco number.

MOROCCO
(*Dance Number*)

MIKE

Kill it, kill it, kill it. This number will never get off the ground.

VICTOR

I don't understand—Joey likes the costumes and flags.

MIKE

Well, use them in that old number of mine—you know—da-da-da—

CHICAGO (MOROCCO)

There's a great big town
On a great big lake
Called Morocco.
When the sun goes down
It is wide awake.
Take your ma and your pa,
Go to Morocco.
—Morocco.

ACT TWO

SCENE IV

The apartment. ERNEST *is fitting new jacket on* JOEY.

JOEY

Wait till my new dance goes in. The Club will be making money then. (*Telephone rings. In phone*) Yeah . . . Who? Why—sure—It's Linda English—It's that girl. You know . . .

VERA

Ask her to come over.

JOEY

Come on over. I don't know what she wants. I haven't seen her.

VERA

Maybe you have, and maybe you haven't. But you're giving your usual impression of a man with a guilty conscience. If your own mother were announced, you'd have a guilty conscience.

JOEY
(*Takes*)

I sure would. Wouldn't you?

VERA

Well, since you put it that way, yes.

JOEY

Although I wouldn't mind if it was my old man. (*Laughs*) He always said I'd never amount to anything.

VERA

What's he doing now?

JOEY

Dads——? Dads is in Palm Beach ...

VERA

Never mind. I'm sorry I asked. You always do everything the hard way.

(JOEY *sings.*)

DO IT THE HARD WAY

Fred Astaire once worked so hard
He often lost his breath,
And now he taps all other chaps to death.
Working hard did not retard
The young Cab Calloway,
Now hear him blow his vo-de-o-do today.

REFRAIN

Do it the hard way
And it's easy sailing.
Do it the hard way
And it's hard to lose.
Only the soft way
Has a chance of failing;
You have to choose.
I took the hard way
When I tried to get you,
You took the soft way

When you said "We'll see."
Darling, now I'll let you
Do it the hard way
Now that you want me.

(*Buzzer.* VERA *rises, eases left.* LINDA *enters right and crosses to* VERA.)

VERA

Hello. How are you?

LINDA

I'm very well, thank you, Mrs. Simpson. Could I speak to you alone?

VERA

Why, of course. (*To* JOEY) Blow, you.

JOEY

Blow?

VERA

Try on one of your new frocks.

JOEY

God, the way you're getting to talk.

VERA

Try on one of your new costumes. (JOEY *exits.* VERA *sits*) I'm sorry I pretended to be a gangster's moll that day.

LINDA
(*Sits*)

Oh, that's all right. I guess I knew you weren't one, but—thats' not what I came to talk about. I came to warm you.

VERA

Warn me? About what?

LINDA

They're going to blackmail you. I overheard them.

VERA

Yes?

LINDA

Oh, you know who they are?

VERA

No. But I have to find out somehow, so I thought I'd let you tell me your own way.

LINDA

(*Rises, crosses to* VERA)

Well, it's that Ludlow Lowell, the agent. And that singer at the club. They have some scheme that they'll tell your husband that you and Mr. Evans—go around together—quite a lot.

VERA

How delicate you are. (*Rises*) Hmmm. What about Joey?

LINDA

Well, they didn't count on getting much out of him. Only all he had.

VERA

I'm afraid his bank balance will be a terrible disappointment. Linda, what about you? Why are you warning me?

LINDA

Why? Because it's dishonest—that's all.

VERA

(*Rises, crosses to* LINDA)

Is it? Is that all? As one woman to another?

LINDA

Well, I certainly hope you don't think it was what you think it was.

VERA

I think it was, though.

LINDA

Well, just don't think it was what you think it was. Take him.

TAKE HIM

LINDA

REFRAIN

> Take him, you don't have to pay for him,
> Take him, he's free.
> Take him, I won't make a play for him,
> He's not for me.
> He has no head to think with,
> True that his heart is asleep.
> But he has eyes to wink with:
> You can have him cheap.
> Keep him, and just for the lure of it,
> Marry him too
> Keep him, for you can be sure of it
> He can't keep you,
> So take my old jalopy,
> Keep him from falling apart.
> Take him, but don't ever take him to heart.

VERA

SECOND CHORUS

> Take him, I won't put a price on him,
> Take him, he's yours.

Take him, pajamas look nice on him,
But how he snores.
Though he is well adjusted,
Certain things make him a wreck.
Last year his arm was busted
Reaching from a check.
His thoughts are seldom consecutive,
He just can't write.
I know a movie executive
Who's twice as bright.
Lots of good luck, you'll need it,
And you'll need aspirin too.
Take him, but don't ever let him take you.

(JOEY *enters in costume at the end of* VERA'S *chorus of "Take Him."*)

JOEY

Well, how do you like it? Who you talking about?

VERA

Linda and I have discovered that we have a mutual friend.

JOEY

Yeah?

VERA

But I don't think you'd recognize him, even if we described him to you.

(*They do harmony half-chorus.*)

TAKE HIM

THIRD CHORUS—HARMONY

I hope that things will go well with him;
I bear no hate.

All I can say is the hell with him,
He gets the gate.
So take my benediction,
Take my old benedict too.
Take it away, it's too good to be true.

(LINDA *exits right.* JOEY *exits, left to change.*
VERA *goes to phone.*)

VERA

Dearborn 3300, please. Speak to Deputy Commissioner O'Brien, please. Mrs. Simpson calling . . . That's
right—Mrs. Prentiss Simpson. Hello, Commissioner?—
You'll get a chance to prove it right now. Yes. Yes, it
is . . . just about the same kind of thing that happened
two years ago. I'm afraid I've been a bad girl again—
not really bad—but just having a little fun—That's
right—What? Well, what's more fun, may I ask?—Oh,
you're slipping. No—I'm not at home. . . . I'm at the
Embassy Arms Apartment—18-B. The name is Evans.
. . . You will?—Oh, thank you—Good-bye. (*Hangs up*)
Dear Jack. What would I do without him? I know
damn well what I'd do. I'd pay. (*Calling off stage,
left*) Beauty!

JOEY
(*Enters*)

Well, what gives?

VERA

I wonder what you did to that girl that made her
like you so much? Or didn't do?

JOEY

I never didn't do anything. Or do anything. I never
nothing.

VERA

Stop that baby-talk. You're a big boy now. Big enough to be blackmailed.

JOEY

Blackmailed? Me? That's for a laugh.

VERA

Laugh now, then, because your friend and agent, Mr. Lowell, and your friend and I don't know what, Miss Gladys Bumps, have a little plan to take me for plenty, and you for whatever you have.

JOEY

Oh, they wouldn't do that. I know they're strictly larceny, but . . .

(*Knock—Buzzer.* JOEY *moves right. Enter* LOWELL *and* GLADYS.)

LOWELL

I took the liberty and assumed the privilege of old acquaintance and came right up without being announced. Do you mind?

JOEY

What do you want?

LOWELL

(*Eases to* JOEY—GLADYS *follows*)

I expected a little more cordiality from client to representative.

GLADYS

I don't like his attitude.

LOWELL

Nor do I, my dear mutton. (*Indicating* GLADYS) But we must proceed. (GLADYS *sits. He crosses to* VERA, *left*) Uh, dear Mrs. Simpson, I bet you're wondering to what you owe the honor of this visit—like in the old plays. Or maybe you're not wondering, but I will tell you. Seating myself on the chaise lounge—(*He does so*) and casually puffing my butt—my object is blackmail.

VERA

Well, I'll be damned.

JOEY

I'll be darned.

LOWELL

I have decided that you are an intelligent woman of the world, Mrs. Simpson. A woman that has been around—not too long, of course ...

VERA

Thanks for that anyway.

LOWELL

Glad to. Now a woman of the world, charming, intelligent, fascinating—she knows that the time comes to pay the piper.

VERA

Did you say viper?

LOWELL

Haw haw haw. Not bad. Not bad. Viper. Vinshield Viper. Like that one? Well, to continue, you know that the day of reckoning must come, and here it is. I reckon $20,000 is a good day's reckoning.

VERA

Twenty thousand.

LOWELL

The way you say it I know we aren't going to have
no trouble, Mrs. Simpson. That's the figure. A little old
twenty thousand.

VERA

Otherwise, I suppose you'll tell my husband that
Joey and I . . .

LOWELL

We would be forced to it, wouldn't we?

VERA

I don't know who'd force you, but I see what you
mean.

JOEY

You'll do that to her over my dead body.

LOWELL

Now Joey, I wouldn't say that if I were you because
on my books you are in hock to me for a little over
seven Gees.

JOEY

What do you mean, "your books?"

LOWELL

My books are better than your books because you
ain't got no books.

JOEY

Why, you lousy . . .

(LOWELL *knocks him out.*)

LOWELL

(*To* VERA *who is at* JOEY's *side*)

We can talk better without him standing there like
a wooden Indian. (*Crosses and looks at* JOEY) Five

short minutes and he'll be as good as new . . . (*Lifts* JOEY *and puts him on couch, left*) . . . so I and you might as well chat.

VERA

Naturally, let's chat. Don't you think twenty thousand is rather high?

LOWELL

Yes. Yes, I do.

VERA

Couldn't we adjust it slightly? We might bargain a little for cash.

LOWELL

Oh, I'm afraid you misunderstood me, or else I didn't make myself clear. I never had no thought about this being anything but a cash deal. From the very beginning I was thinking of cash.

GLADYS

Strictly cash.

LOWELL

Gladys put it correctly. Strictly cash.

VERA

But how am I going to get $20,000 in cash?

GLADYS

Sell some trucks.

LOWELL

Now, Gladys, no more interruptions please. You saw what happened to Joey. There are ways and means of a woman like you getting twenty Gees cash, you know that.

VERA

I haven't got it in the bank.

LOWELL

I hear different. What I hear, I hear you send a check around and deposit it to the Chez Joey account every week without fail.

VERA

Oh. You really made quite a study of this. What am I going to tell my husband when he finds out I have no money in the bank?

LOWELL

Mrs. Simpson, what you oughta be worrying about is what *we're* gonna tell your husband.

VERA

You've got something there. You sure you couldn't come down a little? Say, ten thousand?

LOWELL

I don't see how. You see, Gladys gets her cut out of this. Of course if you could persuade *her* to give up *her* end . . .

GLADYS

Don't even try. Don't waste your time.

LOWELL

Then you see how it is, Mrs. Simpson? I'm afraid we come to the same old dreary sitcheeation, twenty Gees.

(*Phone.*)

VERA

Just a moment . . . Yes, ask her to come up please.

LOWELL

Who was that? We don't want to be interrupted just when we're getting somewhere.

VERA

My hairdresser. She can wait in the next room. The only thing is, Mr. Lowell, I'm about through with Joey anyway.

LOWELL

Mrs. Simpson. Not that I'm a guy that goes around doubting a lady's word but I think you only told me you're through with Joey because you thought you'd bluff me.

VERA

There you're wrong. I've decided he's too expensive. And I'm afraid Joey's eye is beginning to wander. (*Buzzer*) Come in, Jack. You know Mr. Lowell and Miss Bumps?

O'BRIEN
(*Enters*)

Yes, sure, Mrs. Simpson. I'd recognize him in a minute. He used to have his picture in every postoffice in the country. Didn't you Looie?

LOWELL
(*To* GLADYS)

Come on you.

O'BRIEN

You'll blow when I tell you to.

LOWELL

Listen, Copper, we're in the clear. You can't make a pinch here.

O'BRIEN

Who said anything about making a pinch? I just came up here to see you off at the train. You know, Mrs. Simpson, I wouldn't do this for just everybody.

VERA

Mr. Lowell, you see?

LOWELL

Aaah.

O'BRIEN

The shock is too great for him, but he'll have plenty of time to think it over. I guess we go now, Laddie. I have to go with him and see where he buys a ticket for. Come on. Move. Two tickets. You're going too, Gladys.

GLADYS

You and your astrology!

O'BRIEN

Good-bye, Mrs. Simpson. Don't forget the boys at Christmas.

VERA

Especially not this Christmas, Commissioner.

O'BRIEN

Jack.

VERA

Jack. (*To* JOEY) Poor Beauty. You ought to know by this time that chivalry is out of character for you. Never, never do that again.

JOEY
(*Coming out of it*)
Wha—? What'd you say? Ohhh— (*Feels his jaw*)

Hey! What happened? Oh. I know. Did you give him the dough?

VERA

No. You frightened them off.

JOEY

I did? I really frightened them off?—Eh? Well, that Ludlow, not that he isn't a very handy guy with the paws—but you know, he reminds me of a pug I used to know.

VERA

Some other time, Beauty. Right now I have some questions to bother you with. How are you fixed, financially?

JOEY

I got rid of a lot of dough, recently. Why? You want some back?

VERA

No, but I've been thinking. What if I were called away to California, or dropped dead, or something— would you be all right? I mean, for instance, would you eat?

JOEY

Honey Sug, somehow, I always eat. But what's on your mind?

VERA

(*Rises and goes around to console*)

Well, I think I'm going to be called away to California, or maybe drop dead.

JOEY

Come on, say it. This is the brush-off. Those punks gave you a scare, and you're walking out.

VERA

A slightly brutal, though accurate way of putting it.
You can keep the club . . .

JOEY

Are you trying to kid me? You got some other guy,
that's why I'm getting the brusheroo. I get it now—
"Take Him"—you meant me. All right—go on back to
him.

VERA

I have a temper, Beauty, and I want to say a few
things before I lose it.

JOEY

Lose it. It's all you got left to lose.

VERA

(*At phone*)

Dearborn 9900 please. Hello, Commercial National?
I want to speak to Mr. McCrea please. Hello, Harry?
Vera. On that Joey Evans account, no more with-
drawals. If he comes in today, tell him the account's
been closed. And close it.

JOEY

Get out of my apartment.

VERA

Your apartment! (*She crosses down toward him*)
Very well. I won't even wish you all the good luck
you're going to need.

JOEY

Blow.

VERA

Yes, dear.
     (*Sings*):

Wise at last,
My eyes at last
Are cutting you down to your size at last.
Bewitched, bothered and bewildered, no more.
Burned a lot;
But learned a lot.
And now you are broke, though you earned a lot.
Bewitched, bothered and bewildered no more.
Couldn't eat—
Was dyspeptic;
Life was so hard to bear.
Now my heart's antiseptic—
Since he moved out of there.
Romance—finis;
Your chance—finis;
Those ants that invaded my pants—finis—
Bewitched, bothered and bewildered no more.

ACT TWO

SCENE V

PET SHOP. JOEY *is looking through the window toward the pets, smoking a cigarette. He starts off, left, as* LINDA *runs on from left.*

LINDA

Joey, I've been looking all over for you. I spoke to Mrs. Simpson and she said . . .

JOEY

Oh sure, sure—I'm planning on getting out of town.

LINDA

Out of town?

JOEY

New York first—some offer in a musical comedy. They're after me—again.

LINDA

I was hoping you'd come over and have supper at my sister's house. Remember me telling you about my sister.

JOEY

Your sister?

LINDA

Her husband is in the trucking business.

JOEY

Oh sure, sure. Well, maybe next time when I'm passing through. These big New York shows they may bore
me.

LINDA

Won't you please? (*She touches his sleeve.* JOEY
pulls away and turns back to the pets) Well, good-bye.
I guess I'd better be going.

(*She holds hand to* JOEY.)

JOEY

(*Shakes her hand without looking.* LINDA *starts
off.* JOEY *looks up*)
I may shoot you a wire and let you know how things
are.

LINDA

Oh, that would be wonderful. Good-bye.
(*She runs off, left.*)

JOEY

(*Looking after her*)
And thanks, thanks a million.

(*He turns back to the pet shop. A Girl enters
from left, passes* JOEY, *stops and looks at the
pets, then exits right. After she leaves,* JOEY
turns again toward stage left, where LINDA
*exited, moves left, turns slowly and exits right
as the*

Curtain Falls

ABOUT THE AUTHOR

JOHN O'HARA was born in Pottsville, Pennsylvania, in 1905. He wrote numerous novels and story collections, including *Ten North Frederick, A Rage to Live* and *From the Terrace.* He died in 1970.